PENGUIN BOOKS

MAIGRET AT THE CROSSROADS

Georges Simenon was born at Liège in Belgium in
1903. At sixteen he began work as a journalist on
the *Gazette de Liège*. He has published over 190
books, many of them psychological novels, and
others in the Inspector Maigret series, and his work
has been admired by almost all the leading French
and English critics. His books have been translated
into more than twenty-five languages and more than
forty of them have been filmed; his psychological
novels have had a great influence on the French
cinema. He has travelled all over the world, and at
one time lived on a cutter making long journeys of
exploration round the coasts of Northern Europe.
He is married and has four children. His recreations
are riding, fishing, and golf.

GEORGES SIMENON

MAIGRET AT THE CROSSROADS

*

TRANSLATED BY ROBERT BALDICK

PENGUIN BOOKS

Penguin Books Ltd, Harmondsworth, Middlesex, England
Penguin Books Australia Ltd, Ringwood, Victoria, Australia
Penguin Books Canada Ltd, 41 Steelcase Road West, Markham, Ontario, Canada

—

La Nuit du carrefour first published 1931
This translation first published in Penguin Books 1963
Reprinted 1965, 1970, 1972, 1974

—

Copyright © A. Fayard et Cie, 1931
Translation copyright © the Estate of Robert Baldick, 1963

—

Made and printed in Great Britain
by Hazell Watson & Viney Ltd,
Aylesbury, Bucks
Set in Monotype Van Dijck

CHAPTER I

The Black Monocle

WHEN, with a sigh of relief, Maigret pushed his chair back from the desk at which he had been sitting, the interrogation of Carl Andersen had lasted exactly seventeen hours.

Through the uncurtained windows he had seen the crowd of midinettes and office-workers storming the dairy-shops in the Place Saint-Michel at noon, then the bustle dying down, the six o'clock rush towards the Métro and the railway stations, and the dawdling over apéritifs . . .

Mist had covered the Seine. The last tug had gone by, carrying green and red lights and towing three barges. The last bus. The last Métro. The cinema whose grille was closed after the advertisement boards had been taken in . . .

And the stove which seemed to be purring more loudly in Maigret's office. On the table there were some empty beerglasses and the remains of some sandwiches.

A fire must have broken out somewhere, for they heard the noisy fire-engines going past. There was also a raid. The Black Maria drove out of the Prefecture about two o'clock, and came back later by way of the depot yard, where it unloaded its booty.

The interrogation went on and on. Every hour, or every two hours, depending how tired he was, Maigret would press a button. Sergeant Lucas, who was dozing in a near-by office, would come in, glance at the chief-inspector's notes, and take over.

And Maigret would go and lie down on a camp-bed, returning to the attack with new stocks of energy.

The Prefecture was deserted. A few comings and goings in the Vice Squad. A drug pedlar whom an inspector brought in about four o'clock in the morning and started questioning straight away.

The Seine donned a halo of milky mist which turned white, and it was daybreak, lighting up the empty embankments. Footsteps sounded in the corridors. Telephones ringing. Voices calling. Doors banging. The charwomen's brooms.

And Maigret, putting down his overheated pipe on the table, stood up and looked the prisoner over from head to foot, with an irritation not unmixed with admiration.

Seventeen hours of unrelenting interrogation. Beforehand the man's shoelaces, collar, and tie had been removed and his pockets emptied.

During the first four hours he had been left standing in the middle of the office, and questions had been fired as fast as machine-gun bullets.

'Are you thirsty?'

Maigret was on his fourth glass of beer and the prisoner had given a shadow of a smile. He had drunk greedily.

'Are you hungry?'

He had been asked to sit down, then to stand up again. He had gone seven hours with nothing to eat, and after that he had been harried while he was bolting down a sandwich.

There were two of them taking it in turns to question him. Between sessions they could doze, stretch themselves, escape from the obsession of this monotonous interrogation.

And it was they who were giving up! Maigret shrugged his shoulders, looked for a cold pipe in a drawer, wiped his moist forehead.

Perhaps what impressed him most of all was not the man's physical and moral resistance, but the disturbing elegance, the distinction which he retained to the end.

A man of the world who emerges from the search-room without his tie, and who then spends a whole hour, stark naked, with a hundred criminals, in the Records Department,

6

dragged along from the camera to the armchair scales, jostled around, and subjected to the depressing jokes of some of his companions, rarely retains that self-assurance which, in private life, formed part of his personality.

And when he has undergone a few hours of questioning, it is a positive miracle if anything remains to distinguish him from a common tramp.

Carl Andersen had not changed. In spite of his crumpled suit, he still displayed an elegance such as the staff of Police Headquarters rarely have occasion to appreciate, an aristocratic elegance, with that hint of stiffness and restraint, that touch of haughtiness which is the peculiar attribute of diplomatic circles.

He was taller than Maigret, broad-shouldered, but slim, lithe, and narrow-hipped. His long face was pale, his lips rather colourless.

He wore a black monocle in his left eye.

'Take it out,' he had been told.

He had obeyed, with a ghost of a smile. He had uncovered a glass eye of unpleasant fixity.

'An accident?'

'Yes, a flying accident . . .'

'So you were in the war?'

'I'm Danish. I didn't have to fight. But I had a private aircraft back there . . .'

This artificial eye was so embarrassing, in a young face with regular features, that Maigret had growled:

'You can put your monocle back.'

Andersen had not complained once, either that they had kept him standing, or that they had forgotten to give him anything to eat and drink. From his place he could see the people in the street, the trams and buses crossing the bridge, a ray of reddish sunshine towards evening, and now the bustle of a bright April morning.

7

He was still holding himself as erect as ever, without the slightest affectation, and the only sign of fatigue was the deep, narrow shadow underlining his right eye.

'You stand by everything you have told me?'

'I do.'

'You realize how improbable it sounds?'

'Yes, but I can't lie.'

'You hope to be set free, in the absence of positive proof?'

'I don't hope anything.'

A hint of an accent, more pronounced now that he was tired.

'Do you want me to read through the record of your interrogation before asking you to sign it?'

The vague gesture of a man of the world refusing a cup of tea.

'I'll summarize it for you. You arrived in France three years ago, together with your sister Else. You lived for a month in Paris. Then you rented a country house on the main road from Paris to Étampes, two miles from Arpajon, at the place known as the Three Widows Crossroads.'

Carl Andersen nodded in agreement.

'For the past three years you have lived there in the most complete isolation, so complete that the local people have not seen your sister more than two or three times. No contact with your neighbours. You bought a five horse-power motorcar, of an obsolete make, which you use to do your own shopping at the market at Arpajon. Once a month, again in this motor-car, you come to Paris.'

'Yes, that's right, to deliver my work to the firm of Dumas and Son, in the rue du Quatre-Septembre.'

'Work consisting of designs for furnishing fabrics. You are paid five hundred francs for each design. On an average you produce four designs a month, which makes two thousand francs ...'

Another nod.

8

'You have no men friends. Your sister has no women friends. On Saturday night you went to bed as usual at about ten o'clock. And, again as usual, you locked your sister in her bedroom, which is next to yours. You explain that by saying she is very nervous ... let's leave that! ... At seven o'clock on Sunday morning, Monsieur Émile Michonnet, an insurance agent, who lives in a villa a hundred yards from your house, went into his garage and found that his motor-car, a new six-cylinder motor of a well-known make, had disappeared and its place had been taken by your old crock ...'

Andersen did not move, apart from a mechanical gesture towards his empty pocket, in which there must usually have been some cigarettes.

'Monsieur Michonnet, who for some days had been talking about nothing but his new motor all over the place, thought he was the victim of a practical joke. He went over to your house, found the gate locked, and rang the bell without getting any reply. Half an hour later, he related his misfortune to the local police and they went to your house ... They found neither you nor your sister there ... on the other hand, in the garage, they discovered Monsieur Michonnet's motor-car, and in the front seat, slumped over the steering-wheel, a dead man, killed by a shot fired point-blank into his chest ... His papers had not been stolen ... He was a certain Isaac Goldberg, a diamond-merchant from Antwerp ...'

Maigret put some more coke in the stove while he went on talking.

'The local police lost no time in questioning the staff at Arpajon station, who had seen you take the first train for Paris, together with your sister ... The two of you were picked up on your arrival at the Gare d'Orsay ... You deny everything ...'

'I deny having killed anybody ...'

'You also deny having known Isaac Goldberg ...'

'I saw him for the first time, dead, at the wheel of a motor which doesn't belong to me, in my own garage . . .'

'And instead of telephoning the police, you ran for it with your sister . . .'

'I was frightened . . .'

'You've nothing to add?'

'Nothing.'

'And you maintain that you heard nothing during Saturday night?'

'I'm a very heavy sleeper.'

It was the fiftieth time that he had repeated exactly the same phrases, and an exasperated Maigret pressed the electric bell. Sergeant Lucas appeared.

'I'll be back in a moment.'

*

The conversation between Maigret and the examining magistrate Coméliau, to whom the case had been referred, lasted about a quarter of an hour. The magistrate threw in the sponge, so to speak, in advance.

'You'll see, it will be one of those cases which luckily come our way only once every ten years, and which are never solved . . . And they have to pick on me! . . . None of the details makes sense . . . Why were the motor-cars switched? . . . And why didn't Andersen use the one in his garage to get away, instead of walking to Arpajon and taking a train? . . . What was that diamond merchant doing at the Three Widows Crossroads? . . . Take it from me, Maigret, there's a whole string of troubles starting for both of us . . . Let him go if you like . . . You may be right in thinking that if he has stood up to seventeen hours of questioning, there's nothing more to be got out of him . . .'

The Chief-Inspector's eyelids were a little red from lack of sleep.

'Have you seen the sister?'

'No. By the time Andersen was brought along to me, the girl had already been taken home by the local police, who wanted to question her on the spot. She is staying there. She is being watched.'

They shook hands, Maigret went back to his office where Lucas was keeping an indolent eye on the prisoner, who had glued his forehead to the window-pane and was waiting without any sign of impatience.

'You're free!' he said as soon as he opened the door.

Andersen did not give a start, but made a vague gesture towards his bare neck and his gaping shoes.

'Your things will be returned to you at the office. You remain, of course, at the Law's disposal. The slightest attempt at flight, and I'll have you taken to the Santé prison.'

'My sister?'

'You'll find her at home.'

The Dane must have felt some emotion after all as he left the room, for he took out his monocle and passed his hand over his glass eye.

'Thank you, Chief-Inspector.'

'Don't mention it.'

'I give you my word of honour that I'm innocent . . .'

'I'm not asking you for anything!'

Andersen bowed, and waited for Lucas to take him to the office.

Someone had stood up in the waiting-room, had witnessed this scene with astonished indignation, and rushed over to Maigret.

'So you're letting him go? But you can't do that, Chief-Inspector . . .'

It was Monsieur Michonnet, insurance agent, the owner of the new six-cylinder motor-car. He walked arrogantly into the office and put his hat down on a table.

'I've come mainly about the motor.'

A little man with greying hair, dressed with a certain clumsy refinement, and constantly turning up the tips of his waxed moustaches.

He pursed his lips as he spoke, made vague gestures which were intended to be emphatic, picked his words with care.

He was the plaintiff. He was the person the Law was obliged to protect. Was he not a hero of sorts?

He was not the man to allow himself to be overawed. The entire Prefecture was there in order to listen to him.

'I had a long talk last night with Madame Michonnet, whose acquaintance I hope you'll make before long . . . She agrees with me . . . I ought to add that her father was a master at the Montpellier Lycée and that her mother gave piano lessons . . . If I mention that . . . In short . . .'

This was his favourite phrase. He uttered it in a way which was at once curt and condescending.

'In short, a decision must be taken as soon as possible . . . Like everybody else, even rich people like the Comte d'Avrainville, I bought my new motor-car on the instalment system . . . I signed eighteen bills. Mind you, I could have paid cash, but there's no point in immobilizing capital . . . The Comte d'Avrainville, whom I mentioned just now, did the same with his Hispano . . . In short . . .'

Maigret did not move. He was breathing heavily.

'I can't do without a motor. It's absolutely essential for me in the exercise of my profession . . . You see, my area stretches twenty miles from Arpajon . . . Now, Madame Michonnet agrees with me . . . We don't want to keep a motor in which a man has been killed . . . It's up to the Law to do the necessary, to provide us with a new motor, of the same type as the other one, except that I want it to be a maroon shade, which makes no difference to the price . . . You have to remember that my motor had been run in, and I shall have to . . .'

'Is that all you have to say to me?'

'I beg your pardon!'

Another phrase he liked using.

'I beg your pardon, Chief-Inspector! It is understood that I am ready to place all my knowledge and experience of the region at your disposal . . . But it is a matter of urgency that a motor . . .'

Maigret passed his hand over his forehead.

'Very well, I shall come and see you soon at your house . . .'

'And what about the motor?'

'When the investigation is over your motor-car will be returned to you . . .'

'But I told you that Madame Michonnet and I . . .'

'Then give my regards to Madame Michonnet . . . Good morning, Monsieur . . .'

It was done so quickly that the insurance agent had no time to protest. He found himself back on the landing, holding his hat which had been thrust into his hand, while the office messenger was saying: 'This way, please! First staircase on the left . . . The door facing you . . .'

Maigret, for his part, double-locked the door and put some water on the stove to brew himself some strong coffee.

His colleagues thought that he was working. But he had to be woken up when, an hour later, a telegram arrived from Antwerp which said:

Isaac Goldberg, 45, diamond merchant, fairly well known locally. Medium-sized business. Good bank references. Travelled every week, by train or by air, to Amsterdam, London and Paris, canvassing orders.

Luxurious villa rue de Campine, Borgerhout. Married. Two children, 8 and 12.

Madame Goldberg informed. Has taken the Paris train.

*

At eleven o'clock in the morning the telephone rang. It was Lucas.

'Hullo! I'm at the Three Widows Crossroads. I'm phoning to you from the garage two hundred yards from the Andersens' house … The Dane has come home … The gate is locked again … Nothing special to report …'

'The sister?'

'Must be there, but I haven't seen her …'

'Goldberg's body?'

'At the hospital in Arpajon.'

*

Maigret went home to his flat on the Boulevard Richard-Lenoir.

'You look tired!' was all that his wife said to him.

'Pack me a suitcase with a suit and change of socks.'

'Will you be away long?'

There was a stew on the stove. In the bedroom the window was open and the bedclothes thrown back to air the sheets. Madame Maigret had not yet had time to take out the pins which were holding her hair in tight little balls.

'Good-bye …'

He kissed her. Just as he was going out, she remarked:

'You're opening the door with your right hand.'

This was unusual for him. He always opened it with his left hand. And Madame Maigret made no secret of the fact that she was superstitious.

'What is it? A gang?'

'I don't know.'

'Are you going far?'

'I don't know yet.'

'You will take care of yourself, won't you?'

But he was already going downstairs, and he scarcely turned round to wave to her. On the boulevard he hailed a taxi.

'The Gare d'Orsay . . . No, wait . . . How much is it to Arpajon? . . . Three hundred francs, with the return journey? . . . Off we go!'

This rarely happened with him. But he was tired out. He found it hard to drive away the sleep which was making his eyelids prickle.

And then too, perhaps he was a little disturbed. Not so much on account of that door which he had opened with his right hand. Nor on account of that weird story of the motor-car which had been stolen from Michonnet and found again with a dead man at the wheel in Andersen's garage.

It was rather the latter's personality which baffled him.

'Seventeen hours of grilling!'

Experienced criminals, old hands who had been through all the police-stations in Europe, had not stood up to this test.

Perhaps indeed it was for this reason that Maigret had let Andersen go.

All the same, after Bourg-la-Reine he fell asleep in the back of the taxi. The driver woke him up at Arpajon, in front of the old market with the thatched roof.

'Which hotel are you stopping at?'

'Go on to the Three Widows Crossroads . . .'

Up a hill, along the main road glistening with oil and lined on both sides with hoardings advertising Vichy, Deauville, big hotels, or brands of petrol.

A crossroads. A garage and its five petrol-pumps, painted red. On the left the road to Avrainville, marked by a signpost.

All around, fields as far as the eye could see.

'Here we are,' said the driver.

There were only three houses. First the garage proprietor's, in plaster tiles, run up in a speculative fever. A big sports model, with aluminium coach-work, was being filled up. Some mechanics were repairing a butcher's van.

Facing the garage, a villa in millstone grit, with a narrow

garden, surrounded by railings six feet high. A brass plate: ÉMILE MICHONNET. INSURANCE AGENT.

The other house was two hundred yards away. The wall surrounding the park allowed only a glimpse of the first floor, a slate roof, and a few imposing trees.

This last building was at least a hundred years old. It was the traditional country house of former times, including a lodge for the gardener, outbuildings, poultry-houses, a stable, and a flight of five steps flanked by bronze statues carrying torches.

There was a little cement pond which was bone-dry. A thin wisp of smoke was rising straight into the air from a chimney with a carved cornice.

That was all. Beyond the fields, a rock, some farmhouse roofs, a plough left somewhere on the edge of the fields.

And on the smooth road, motor-cars going by, sounding their horns, passing, overtaking.

Maigret got out of the taxi, holding his suitcase, and paid the driver, who, before setting off on the return journey to Paris, bought some petrol at the garage.

CHAPTER 2

The Curtains Which Moved

LUCAS emerged from one of the shoulders of the road, whose trees had been concealing him, and came over to Maigret who was putting his suitcase down at his feet. Just as they were going to shake hands they heard a whistling sound growing into a screech and suddenly a sports model passed the two men at top speed, so close that the suitcase was flung three yards away.

They did not see anything. The motor-car with the turbo-compressor overtook a haycart and disappeared over the horizon.

Maigret pulled a face.

'Do many go by like that?'

'It's the first ... You'd have sworn it was aiming at us, wouldn't you?'

It was a grey afternoon. A curtain quivered in one of the windows of the Michonnet villa.

'Is it possible to stay anywhere here?'

'At Arpajon or at Avrainville ... Arpajon is a couple of miles away ... Avrainville is nearer, but you'll find nothing there but a country inn.'

'Take my suitcase over there and book a couple of rooms ... Nothing to report?'

'Not a thing ... We are being watched from the villa ... It's Madame Michonnet, whom I examined a little earlier on ... A rather buxom brunette, who can't be very good-natured ...'

'Do you know why they call this place the Three Widows Crossroads?'

'I asked about that . . . It's on account of the Andersens' house . . . It dates back to the Revolution . . . In the old days it was the only building at the crossroads . . . Fifty years ago, it seems it was occupied by three widows, a mother, and her two daughters. The mother was ninety years old and bed-ridden. The elder daughter was sixty-seven and the other a good sixty. Three old cranks, so mean that they bought nothing in the neighbourhood and lived on the produce of their kitchen-garden and their poultry-yard . . . The shutters were never opened. Weeks went by without anybody catching a glimpse of them . . . The elder daughter broke her leg and nobody knew about it until she was dead . . . A queer story! . . . For a long time nobody had heard the slightest noise coming from the house of the Three Widows . . . So people started talking . . . The mayor of Avrainville decided to have a look . . . He found them dead, all three of them, dead for at least ten days! . . . I was told that the papers talked a lot about it at the time . . . A local schoolteacher, who was fascinated by the mystery, even wrote a booklet about it in which he claimed that the daughter with the broken leg, out of hatred for her sister who was still agile, poisoned her, and that the mother was poisoned at the same time . . . Then she died beside the two corpses, because she couldn't move to get something to eat!'

Maigret gazed at the house of which he could see only the upper part, then looked at the Michonnets' new villa, the even newer garage, and the traffic going past along the main road at fifty miles an hour.

'Go and book those rooms . . . Then come back and join me.'

'What are you going to do?'

The Chief-Inspector shrugged his shoulders, and first of all walked over to the gate of the house of the Three Widows. It was a roomy building, surrounded by a park of eight or nine acres planted with a few magnificent trees.

A sloping drive went round a lawn, leading to the front door on the one hand, and on the other to a garage fitted up inside a former stable whose roof was still adorned with a pulley.

Nothing stirred. Apart from the wisp of smoke, there was no sign of life behind the faded curtains. Dusk was beginning to fall and some horses were crossing a distant field on their way back to the farm.

Maigret saw a little man walking along the road, his hands in the pockets of a pair of flannel trousers, a pipe between his teeth, a cap on his head. This man came up to him familiarly, in the way neighbours accost one another in the country.

'Are you the fellow in charge of the case?'

He had no collar. He was wearing slippers. But his jacket was a fine grey English cloth and he had a huge signet-ring on one finger.

'I run the garage at the crossroads . . . I saw you from over there.'

A former boxer, that was certain. His nose had been broken. His face was so to speak hammer-wrought by other men's fists. His drawling voice was hoarse and vulgar, but full of confidence.

'What do you think of this business of the motor-cars?'

He laughed, revealing several gold teeth.

'If it wasn't for the fact that there's a corpse involved, I'd find it damn funny . . . You can't understand! You don't know the fellow across the road, *Mossieu* Michonnet as we call him . . . A gent who doesn't like you to be too pally, who wears stiff collars as high as that, and patent-leather shoes . . . And Madame Michonnet! . . . You haven't seen her yet? . . . Hmm! . . . Those two kick up a fuss over anything and everything, and go for the police because the motors make too much noise when they stop in front of my petrol-pump . . .'

Maigret looked at the man without encouraging him or

discouraging him. He just looked at him, which was upsetting for most gossips but was not enough to put off the garage-proprietor.

A baker's van went by and the man in the slippers shouted:

'Evening, Clément! . . . Your horn's ready . . . Just ask Jojo for it.'

Turning to Maigret and offering him a cigarette, he went on:

'For months he talked about buying a new motor and pestered all the dealers, including me . . . He wanted a reduction in price . . . He made us sweat . . . The coachwork was too dark or too light . . . He wanted a plain claret, but not too claret, though claret all the same . . . To cut a long story short, he ended up by buying it from a colleague of mine at Arpajon . . . You must admit it was a hell of a joke finding the motor a few days later in the Three Widows' garage! . . . I'd have given a lot to see the fellow's face in the morning when he saw the old crock in the place of his six-cylinder! . . . A pity about the corpse – it spoils everything . . . Because when all's said and done a corpse is a corpse, and after all you've got to show a bit of respect for that sort of thing . . . I say, you'll drop in to the garage for a drink, won't you? . . . We're a bit short of pubs at the crossroads . . . But that will come! Just wait until I find a good chap to run it and I'll give him the capital . . .'

The man must have seen that his words were producing hardly any response, for he held his hand out to Maigret.

'See you later . . .'

He ambled off, stopping to talk to a peasant who was passing by in a cart. There was still a face behind Michonnet's curtains. In the evening light the country on both sides of the road had a monotonous, stagnant look, and sounds could be heard from a long way off: the neighing of a horse, a church-bell which might have been five or six miles away.

A motor-car went by with its headlamps on, but they scarcely showed in the half-light.

Maigret reached for the bell-pull which hung to the right of the gate. A fine, solemn peal rang out in the garden, followed by a long silence. The door at the top of the flight of steps did not open. But there was a crunch of gravel behind the house. A tall silhouette appeared, a milky-white face, a black monocle.

Without any apparent emotion, Carl Andersen came up to the gate, unlocked it, and bowed his head.

'I imagined you would be coming . . . I suppose you want to see the garage . . . The Public Prosecutor's department have put seals on it, but you must have authority to . . .'

He was wearing the same suit as at the Quai des Orfèvres, a suit of impeccable cut which was beginning to get a little shiny.

'Is your sister here?'

It was already too dark to make out any quivering of the features, but Andersen felt the need to screw his monocle more firmly in his eye.

'Yes.'

'I should like to see her . . .'

A slight hesitation. A fresh bow of the head.

'Please follow me . . .'

They went round the building. Behind it stretched a fairly large lawn overlooked by a terrace. All the ground-floor rooms had tall french windows which opened straight on to this terrace.

There was no light in any of the bedrooms. At the far end of the park, swathes of mist veiled the tree trunks.

'Allow me to lead the way.'

Andersen pushed open a french window and Maigret followed him into a big drawing-room padded with shadows. The window was left open, letting in the cool yet heavy air of

21

evening, as well as a smell of wet grass and leaves. A solitary log was throwing off a few sparks in the fireplace.

'I'll go and call my sister.'

Andersen had not lighted a lamp, had not even seemed to notice that the dusk was falling. Maigret, left on his own, paced slowly up and down the room, and stopped in front of an easel holding a gouache sketch. It was a sketch for a modern fabric, with bold colours and a strange pattern.

But not as strange as the room itself, in which Maigret found echoes of the three widows of old.

Some of the furniture must have belonged to them. There were some Empire armchairs with flaking paint and worn silk, and rep curtains which had not been taken down for fifty years.

On the other hand some deal bookshelves had been built along one wall, which were stacked with paperbacked books in French, German, English, and presumably Danish too.

And the white, yellow, or multicoloured covers contrasted sharply with an old-fashioned tuffet, some chipped vases, and a carpet which was threadbare in the middle.

The twilight deepened. A cow lowed in the distance. And every now and then a faint hum broke the silence, grew steadily louder, a motor-car roared past along the road, and the sound of the engine died away.

Inside the house, there was nothing to be heard. At the most a few creaking or scratching sounds. At the most a few tiny, unrecognizable noises, hinting at the existence of some life.

Carl Andersen came in first. His white hands betrayed a certain nervousness. He said nothing, and stood motionless for a moment by the door.

A gentle movement on the stairs.

'My sister Else,' he announced at last.

She came forward, the outlines of her figure blurred in the

half-light. She came forward like a film star, or rather like the ideal woman in an adolescent's dream.

Was her dress made of black velvet? In any case it was darker than the rest, forming a deep, rich patch. And what little light still remained scattered in the air concentrated on her fine fair hair, on her lustreless face.

'I gather that you wish to speak to me, Chief-Inspector . . . But first of all please sit down . . .'

Her accent was more pronounced than Carl's. Her voice sang, dropping on the last syllable of the longer words.

And her brother stood beside her like a slave standing beside a ruler whom it is his duty to protect.

She took a few steps forward, and it was only when she was very close that Maigret realized that she was as tall as Carl. Her slim hips lent added emphasis to the lithe grace of her figure.

'A cigarette!' she said, turning to her brother.

He obeyed her, showing a certain clumsiness in his anxiety. She used a cigarette-lighter which she picked up from a piece of furniture, and for a moment the red of the flame warred with the dark blue of her eyes.

Afterwards the darkness was more noticeable, so noticeable that the Chief-Inspector, feeling ill at ease, looked for a light-switch, failed to find one, and murmured:

'May I ask you to light a lamp?'

He needed all the composure he could command. This scene was too theatrical for his liking. Theatrical? Too oppressive, rather, like the scent which had filled the room since Else had come in.

Above all, too foreign to everyday life. Or perhaps just simply too foreign.

That accent . . . That impeccable distinction of Carl's and his black monocle . . . That mixture of luxury and appalling old rubbish . . . Even Else's dress, which was not the sort of dress one saw in the street, or at the theatre, or in society . . .

What was there about it that was different? Probably the way she wore it. For the cut was simple. The material fitted her body tightly and even covered her neck, revealing nothing but her face and hands . . .

Andersen had bent over a table and was removing the chimney from an oil-lamp dating back to the three old women, a lamp with a porcelain stand decorated with imitation bronze.

It made a ring of light six feet across in one corner of the drawing-room. The shade was orange.

'Excuse me . . . I hadn't noticed that all the chairs were cluttered up.'

And Andersen cleared an Empire armchair of the books which were piled in it. He put them in an untidy heap on the carpet. Else stood smoking her cigarette, an erect figure sculptured by the velvet.

'Your brother, Mademoiselle, has told me that he heard nothing unusual during Saturday night . . . It seemed that he is a very heavy sleeper . . .'

'Very,' she repeated, exhaling a little smoke.

'You heard nothing either?'

'Nothing particularly unusual, no.'

She spoke slowly, like a foreigner who had to translate phrases conceived in her own language.

'You know that we live on a main road. The traffic scarcely slackens during the night. Every day, from eight o'clock in the evening, lorries go past on their way to the Central Market in Paris and make a lot of noise. On Saturday there are also the tourists making for the Loire and Sologne . . . Our sleep is interrupted all the time by the noises of engines and brakes and loud voices . . . If the house were not so cheap . . .'

'You have never heard of Goldberg?'

'Never . . .'

The darkness outside was not yet complete. The lawn was a uniform green, and one had the impression that one could have counted the blades of grass, they stood out so clearly.

The park, despite the lack of upkeep, remained as harmonious as an operatic stage-set. Every clump of shrubs, every tree, indeed every branch was exactly where it should be. And a horizon of fields, together with a farmhouse roof, completed this sort of Île-de-France symphony.

In the drawing-room, on the other hand, in the midst of the old furniture there were spires of foreign books, there were words which Maigret did not understand. And these two foreigners, the brother and the sister, especially the latter, who struck a discordant note . . .

A note which was too voluptuous, too lascivious perhaps? But there was nothing provocative about her. All her gestures and postures were simple.

But their simplicity was not that which the setting called for. The Chief-Inspector would have felt more at ease with the three old women and their monstrous passions!

'Will you allow me to look round the house?'

Neither Carl nor Else showed the slightest hesitation. It was he who picked up the lamp, while she sat down in an armchair.

'If you will follow me . . .'

'I suppose you use this drawing-room most of the time?'

'Yes. It's here that I do my work and my sister spends most of her time . . .'

'You haven't any servants?'

'You know now how much I earn. It isn't enough to allow me to pay a servant.'

'Who does the cooking?'

'I do.'

He said this simply, without any embarrassment or shame,

and as the two men reached a corridor, Andersen pushed open a door, raised the lamp to light up the kitchen, and said primly:

'Please excuse the untidiness . . .'

It was more than untidiness. It was sordid. A spirit stove caked with boiled milk, sauce, and fat, on a table a scrap of oilcloth. Some bits of bread. A piece of collop in a frying-pan left on the table, and dirty crockery in the sink.

When they were back in the corridor, Maigret glanced towards the drawing-room, where there was no longer any light and nothing could be seen but the glow of Else's cigarette.

'We don't use the dining-room or the little drawing-room at the front of the house. Do you want to have a look?'

The lamp lit up a rather pretty parquet, pieces of furniture piled on top of one another, and potatoes scattered about on the floor. The shutters were closed.

'Our bedrooms are upstairs . . .'

The staircase was wide. One step creaked. The scent became stronger, the higher they went.

'This is my room . . .'

Just a spring-mattress laid on the floor to serve as a divan. A rudimentary dressing-table. A big Louis Quinze wardrobe. An ashtray overflowing with cigarette-ends.

'You smoke a lot?'

'In the morning, in bed . . . Perhaps thirty cigarettes while I'm reading . . .'

Outside the door opposite his, he said very quickly:

'My sister's room . . .'

But he did not open it. He scowled while Maigret turned the handle and pushed the door open.

Andersen was still holding the lamp and he avoided bringing the light nearer. The scent was so overpowering that it took one by the throat.

The whole house was lacking in style, order, luxury. It was a camping ground full of old odds and ends.

But here, in the half-light, the chief-inspector sensed something in the nature of a warm, luxurious oasis. The floor could not be seen for it was covered with animal skins, including a magnificent tiger-skin which served as a bedside rug.

The bed itself was made of ebony, covered with black velvet. On this velvet, some crumpled silk underwear.

Andersen was imperceptibly moving away with the lamp down the corridor, and Maigret followed him.

'There are three other bedrooms, all empty . . .'

'So that your sister's room is the only one that looks out on the road . . .'

Carl made no reply, but pointed to a narrow staircase.

'The backstairs . . . We don't use them . . . If you want to see the garage . . .'

They went downstairs, one behind the other, in the dancing light of the oil-lamp. In the drawing-room the red dot of a cigarette was still the only illumination.

As Andersen went forward, the light invaded the room. Else was revealed, lying back in an armchair, her eyes gazing indifferently at the two men.

'You haven't offered the Chief-Inspector a cup of tea, Carl!'

'Thank you, but I never drink tea . . .'

'But I do, and I want some now! Will you have some whisky? Or else . . . Carl! Please . . .'

And Carl, confused and nervous, put the lamp down and lit a little spirit stove which stood underneath a silver teapot.

'What can I offer you, Chief-Inspector?'

Maigret could not manage to identify the source of his uneasiness. The atmosphere was at once cosy and untidy. Big flowers with purplish-blue petals were blossoming on the easel.

'In short,' he said 'somebody stole Monsieur Michonnet's

motor-car to begin with. Goldberg was murdered in that motor, which was then driven into your garage. And your motor was driven into the insurance-agent's garage.'

'It's incredible, isn't it?'

Else spoke with a soft, lilting voice, while lighting another cigarette.

'My brother insisted that we should be accused because the dead man was found in our garage ... He wanted to run away ... I didn't want to ... I was sure that the police would understand that if we had really committed the murder, it would not be in our interest to ...'

She broke off and looked round for Carl who was rummaging in a corner.

'Well, aren't you going to offer anything to the Chief-Inspector?'

'I'm sorry ... I ... I've just found there isn't any left ...'

'You're always the same! You never think of anything ... You must forgive us, Monsieur ...?'

'Maigret.'

'... Monsieur Maigret ... We drink very little spirits and ...'

There was the sound of footsteps in the park where Maigret made out the figure of Sergeant Lucas looking for him.

CHAPTER 3

The Night at the Crossroads

'WHAT is it, Lucas?'

Maigret was standing at the french window. Behind him he had the uneasy atmosphere of the drawing-room, in front of him Lucas's face in the cool shadows of the park.

'Nothing, Chief-Inspector . . . I was looking for you . . .'

And a rather embarrassed Lucas tried to look into the room, over the Chief-Inspector's shoulders.

'You've booked a room for me?'

'Yes . . . There's a telegram for you . . . Madame Goldberg is arriving tonight by motor-car . . .'

Maigret turned round, and saw Andersen waiting with bowed head, Else smoking and swinging one foot impatiently.

'I shall probably come back tomorrow to go on questioning you,' he told them. 'My respects, Mademoiselle . . .'

She nodded to him with gracious condescension. Carl offered to see the two police officers to the gate.

'You aren't going to look at the garage?'

'Tomorrow . . .'

'Listen, Chief-Inspector . . . What I'm going to say may strike you as rather strange . . . I should like to ask you to make use of me if I can be of service in any way . . . I know that I'm a foreigner, and that apart from that I am the person held in most suspicion . . . All the more reason why I should do my utmost to help find the murderer . . . Please don't hold my clumsiness against me . . .'

Maigret looked him straight in the eyes. He saw one sad

pupil which turned slowly aside. Carl Andersen locked the gate behind them and went back to the house.

*

'What got into you, Lucas?'

'I wasn't easy in my mind . . . It's some time since I got back from Avrainville . . . I don't know why, but all of a sudden this crossroads seemed to have an ugly look about it . . .'

The two of them were walking in the dark along the shoulder of the road. The passing motor-cars were few and far between.

'I've tried to reconstruct the crime in my mind,' he went on, 'and the more you think about it, the more fantastic it seems.'

They had come abreast of the Michonnets' villa, which was so to speak one point of a triangle whose other angles were formed, on the one hand by the garage, on the other hand by the house of the Three Widows. Forty yards between the garage and the Michonnets. A hundred yards between the latter and the Andersens.

Linking them together, the shining, even ribbon of the road embanked like a river by tall trees.

There was no light to be seen in the direction of the Three Widows. Two windows were lit up in the insurance agent's house, but dark curtains let out only a strip of light, an uneven strip which showed that somebody was parting the curtains at eye level in order to look outside.

In the direction of the garage, the milky discs of the petrol-pumps, and also a rectangle of glaring light coming from the workshop in which hammering could be heard.

The two men had halted and Lucas, who was one of Maigret's oldest colleagues, explained.

'First of all, Goldberg had to get here. You've seen the corpse, in the mortuary at Étampes? No? . . . A man of forty-five, with a pronounced Jewish look. A stocky little fellow,

30

with a tough jaw, a stubborn forehead and frizzy hair ... A showy suit ... Fine linen bearing his monogram ... A man accustomed to living well, giving orders, spending freely ... No mud or dust on his patent-leather shoes ... So, even if he came to Arpajon by train, he didn't walk the two miles from the town.

'My theory is that he came from Paris, perhaps even from Antwerp, in a motor ...

'The doctor states that the digestion of his dinner was complete at the time of death, which was instantaneous ... On the other hand, in his stomach they found quite a considerable amount of champagne and grilled almonds.

'At Arpajon, no hotel proprietor sold any champagne on Saturday night, and I defy you to find any grilled almonds anywhere in the town ...'

A lorry went past at thirty miles an hour with a rattle of old iron.

'Look at the Michonnets' garage, Chief-Inspector. The insurance agent has only had a motor for a year. His first was an old crock, and the only shelter he bothered to give it was that wooden shed which has a padlock on the door and opens on to the road. He hasn't had time to have another garage built since then. So it's there that the murderer went to get the new six-cylinder. He had to drive it over to the house of the Three Widows, open the gate, open the garage, take out Andersen's old crock, put Michonnet's motor in its place ... And, on top of all that, install Goldberg at the wheel and kill him with a shot fired at point-blank range ... Nobody saw anything or heard anything! ... *Nobody has an alibi!* ... I don't know if you have the same impression, but coming back from Avrainville just now, in the falling dusk, I felt non-plussed ... It seemed to me that the case looked all wrong, that there was something unnatural, almost treacherous about it ...

'I went up to the gate of the house of the Three Widows ... I knew you were in there ... The front of the house was dark, but I could make out a yellowish glow in the garden ...

'It's idiotic, I know, but I was afraid! ... Afraid for you, I mean ... Don't turn round too quickly ... It's Madame Michonnet who's stationed behind her curtains ...

'I must be mistaken ... And yet I'd swear that half the drivers who go past look at us in a special way...'

Maigret's gaze swept round the triangle. He could no longer see the fields, which had been swallowed up by the darkness. On the right of the main road, opposite the garage, the road to Avrainville branched off, not flanked with trees like the highway, but bordered on one side only by a line of telegraph posts.

Eight hundred yards away, a few lights: the first houses in the village.

'Champagne and grilled almonds!' muttered the Chief-Inspector.

He started walking slowly, only to stop outside the garage where, in the bright light of an arc-lamp, a mechanic in overalls was changing a wheel on a motor-car.

It was more a repair-shop than a garage. It contained about a dozen motors, all of them ancient and old-fashioned, and one of them, stripped of its wheels and its engine, and reduced to the state of a carcass, was hanging from the chains of a pulley.

'Let's go and have dinner! What time is Madame Goldberg due to arrive?'

'I don't know ... During the evening ...'

*

The inn at Avrainville was empty. A zinc counter, a few bottles, a large stove, a small billiard-table, its cloth torn and its cushions as hard as iron, a cat and a dog lying side by side ...

The proprietor waited on the two men, while his wife could be seen grilling some collops in the kitchen.

'What's the name of the man who runs the garage at the crossroads?' asked Maigret, swallowing a sardine which was doing duty as *hors-d'œuvre*.

'Monsieur Oscar . . .'

'Has he lived here for long?'

'Maybe eight years . . . Maybe ten . . . I've got a horse and cart, I have, so . . .'

And the man went on serving them in a half-hearted manner. He was no talker. He even had the sly look of somebody on his guard.

'And Monsieur Michonnet?'

'He's the insurance agent . . .'

That was all.

'White wine or red?'

He wasted a lot of time trying to extract a piece of cork which had fallen into the bottle, and ended up by decanting the wine.

'And the people in the house of the Three Widows?'

'I've never really seen them . . . Not the lady, anyway, because it seems there's a lady there . . . The main road isn't Avrainville after all . . .'

'Well done?' his wife shouted from the kitchen.

Maigret and Lucas ended up by saying nothing, each following the train of his thoughts. At nine o'clock, after drinking a synthetic calvados, they went back to the main road, walked up and down for a while, and finally set off towards the crossroads.

'She's taking a long time.'

'I'd like to know what brought Goldberg here . . . Champagne and grilled almonds! . . . Did they find any diamonds in his pockets?'

'No . . . Just a little over two thousand francs in his wallet.'

The garage was still lit up. Maigret noted that Monsieur Oscar's house was not at the edge of the road but stood behind the workshop, so that it was impossible to see its windows.

The mechanic in overalls was sitting eating on the running-board of a motor-car. And suddenly the garage-proprietor himself emerged from the shadows of the road, a few feet away from the police officers.

'Good evening, gentlemen!'

'Good evening,' grunted Maigret.

'A lovely night! If it keeps this up, we'll have splendid weather for Easter . . .'

'Tell me,' the Chief-Inspector said bluntly, 'does your shop stay open all night?'

'Open, no! But there's always a man on duty, who sleeps on a camp-bed. The door is locked . . . People who know the place ring the bell if they need anything . . .'

'Is there much traffic on the road at night?'

'Not a lot. But there is some, all the same . . . Lorries on their way to the Central Market . . . This is the country for early vegetables and especially for watercress . . . The drivers sometimes run out of petrol . . . Or else there's a minor repair that needs doing . . . Won't you come in and have a drink?'

'No, thanks.'

'Pity . . . But I won't press you . . . So you haven't solved that business of the motors yet? . . . You know, it's going to make Monsieur Michonnet downright ill! . . . Especially if he doesn't get a six-cylinder back straight away!'

A headlamp shone in the distance, grew larger. A roar. A shadow went by.

'The doctor from Étampes,' murmured the garage-proprietor. 'He's been seeing a patient at Arpajon. His colleague must have kept him for dinner . . .'

'You know all the vehicles that go past here?'

'A lot of them . . . Look at those two side-lamps, for instance . . . That's a lorry-load of cress for the Central Market . . . Those chaps can never bring themselves to light their headlamps . . . And they take up the whole width of the road! . . . Evening, Jules! . . .'

A voice replied from the cab of the passing lorry, and then there was nothing to be seen but the little red rear-light, which was soon swallowed up in the darkness.

A train somewhere, a luminous caterpillar which stretched itself out in the chaos of the night.

'The 9.32 express . . . You're sure you won't have anything? . . . Hey there, Jojo! . . . When you've finished eating, check the third pump, will you? It's broken down . . .'

More headlamps. But the motor went past. It was not Madame Goldberg.

Maigret was smoking all the time. Leaving Monsieur Oscar outside his garage, he started walking up and down, followed by Lucas who was talking quietly to himself.

No light in the house of the Three Widows. The detectives passed the gate a dozen times. Every time Maigret automatically looked up at the window which he knew to be that of Else's room.

Then came the Michonnets' villa, brand-new and devoid of personality, with its varnished oak door and its ridiculous little garden.

Then the garage, the mechanic busy repairing the petrol-pump, and Monsieur Oscar giving him advice, both hands in his pockets.

A lorry from Étampes on its way to Paris stopped to fill up with petrol. On top of the pile of vegetables a man was lying asleep, a driver's mate who travelled the same road every night at the same time.

'Thirty litres.'

'All right?'

'All right.'

The noise of the clutch being let in, and the lorry moved away, going downhill towards Arpajon at forty miles an hour.

'She won't be coming now,' sighed Lucas. 'Probably she decided to spend the night in Paris . . .'

They covered the two hundred yards to the crossroads another three times, then Maigret suddenly made off in the direction of Avrainville. When he arrived in front of the inn, all the lamps were out except one, and there was nobody to be seen in the café.

'I think I can hear a motor.'

They turned round. It was true. A couple of headlamps were piercing the darkness in the direction of the village. A motor-car was obviously turning slowly opposite the garage. Someone was talking.

'They're asking their way.'

The motor finally drew near, lighting up the telegraph posts one after another. Maigret and Lucas were caught in the beam of light, both of them standing in front of the inn.

The sound of brakes. A chauffeur got out and walked round to the door, which he opened.

'You are sure it is here?' a woman's voice asked from inside.

'Yes, Madame. Avrainville . . . And there's a branch of fir over the door . . .'

A silk-stockinged leg. A foot was placed on the ground. There was a glimpse of fur. Maigret started to walk towards the visitor.

At that moment there was an explosion, a cry, the woman fell headlong, literally crashed on to the ground, and there she stayed, rolled up in a ball, while one of her legs kicked out in a spasm.

*

The Chief-Inspector and Lucas looked at one another.

'See to her!' shouted Maigret.

But already a few seconds had been lost. The chauffeur, utterly dumbfounded, stood rooted to the spot. A window opened on the first floor of the inn.

The shot had come from the field on the right of the road. As he ran along the Chief-Inspector drew his revolver from his pocket. He could hear something, a soft thud of footsteps in the clay. But he could not see anything, on account of the motor's headlamps, which, flooding part of the scene with glaring light, made the darkness everywhere else complete.

He turned round and shouted: 'The headlamps!'

At first nothing happened. He repeated his call. And then there was a disastrous misunderstanding. The chauffeur or Lucas turned on the headlamps in the direction of the Chief-Inspector.

The result was that the latter was silhouetted, huge and black, on the bare ground of the field.

The murderer must have been farther on, or more to the left, or more to the right, outside the circle of light in any case.

'The headlamps, dammit!' Maigret yelled for the last time.

His fists were clenched with rage. He was running in zig-zags, like a hunted rabbit. Because of the light, the notion of distance itself was lost, so that all of a sudden he saw the garage's pumps less than a hundred yards away.

Then there was a human form, very close to him, a hoarse voice asking: 'What's the matter?'

Maigret stopped short, furious, humiliated, looked Monsieur Oscar over from head to foot, and saw that there was no mud on his slippers.

'You haven't seen anybody.'

'Just a motorist who asked the way to Avrainville . . .'

The Chief-Inspector caught sight of a red lamp on the main road, in the direction of Arpajon.

'What's that?'

'A lorry for the Central Market.'

'Did it stop here?'

'Long enough to fill up with twenty litres.'

There was considerable activity over by the inn, and the headlamps were still sweeping the empty field.

Maigret suddenly noticed the Michonnets' house, crossed the road, and rang the bell.

A little spy-hole opened.

'Who's there?'

'Chief-Inspector Maigret ... I should like to speak to Monsieur Michonnet ...'

A chain was undone, two bolts pulled back. A key turned in the lock. Madame Michonnet appeared, looking worried, even distracted, and in spite of herself darted furtive glances along the road, in both directions.

'You haven't seen him?'

'You mean he isn't here?' growled Maigret, with a gleam of hope.

'That's to say ... I don't know ... I ... Somebody's just fired a shot, haven't they? ... But come in!'

She was about forty, and had an unattractive face, with prominent features.

'Monsieur Michonnet went out for a moment to ...'

A door was open on the left, the door into the dining-room. The table had not been cleared.

'How long is it since he went out?'

'I don't know ... Perhaps half an hour ...'

Something moved in the kitchen.

'Have you got a maid?'

'No ... It may be the cat ...'

The Chief-Inspector opened the door and saw Monsieur Michonnet himself who was coming by the garden door. His shoes were caked with mud. He was mopping his forehead.

There was a silence, a moment of astonishment, during which the two men looked at one another.

'Your gun!' said the detective.

'My what?'

'Your gun! Quick!'

The insurance agent held out to him a little revolver which he had taken from one of his trouser pockets. But the six bullets were all in it. The barrel was cold.

'Where have you come from?'

'Over there . . .'

'What do you mean by over there?'

'Don't be frightened, Émile! . . . They wouldn't dare do anything to you!' interrupted Madame Michonnet. 'This really is too much . . . And when I think that my brother-in-law is a justice of the peace at Carcassonne . . .'

'Just a moment, Madame . . . I'm talking to your husband . . . You've just come from Avrainville . . . What were you doing there?'

'Avrainville? . . . Me? . . .'

He was trembling. He tried in vain to show a bold front. But his astonishment seemed to be genuine.

'I swear I've been over there, at the house of the Three Widows . . . I wanted to keep an eye on them myself, seeing that . . .'

'You didn't go into the field? . . . You didn't hear anything?'

'There was a shot, wasn't there? . . . Has somebody been killed?'

His moustache was drooping. He looked at his wife as a little boy looks at his mother in time of danger.

'I swear to you, Chief-Inspector! . . . I swear to you . . .'

He stamped on the floor, while a couple of tears started from his eyes.

'It's absolutely monstrous!' he burst out. 'It's my motor

that is stolen! It's in my motor that somebody leaves a corpse! And then they refuse to let me have it back, when I've slaved away for fifteen years to buy it! . . . And now it's me they accuse of . . .'

'Be quiet, Émile! . . . I'll speak to him!'

But Maigret did not give her time.

'There are no other weapons in the house?'

'No, just this revolver, which we bought when we had the villa built . . . And then the bullets are the ones the gunsmith put in himself . . .'

'You've been at the house of the Three Widows?'

'I was afraid that my motor might be stolen again . . . I wanted to carry out my own investigation . . . I went into the park, or to be precise I climbed the wall . . .'

'You saw them?'

'Whom? . . . The pair? . . . The Andersens? . . . Of course! . . . They're there in the sitting-room . . . They've been quarrelling for the past hour . . .'

'Had you left when you heard the shot?'

'Yes . . . but I wasn't sure that it was a shot . . . I just thought so . . . I was worried . . .'

'You saw nobody else?'

'Nobody . . .'

Maigret walked to the door. When he opened it he found Monsieur Oscar coming towards him.

'Your colleague sent me, Chief-Inspector, to tell you the woman is dead . . . My mechanic has gone to tell the police at Arpajon . . . He'll bring a doctor back with him . . . Will you excuse me? I can't leave the garage unattended . . .'

At Avrainville the pale headlamps could still be seen lighting up part of one wall of the inn, and shadows moving around a motor-car.

CHAPTER 4

The Prisoner

MAIGRET was walking slowly, his head bowed, across the field in which the corn was beginning to speckle the earth with pale green.

It was morning. There was some sunshine and the air was vibrant with the singing of invisible birds. In front of the inn at Avrainville, Lucas was waiting for the officials from the Public Prosecutor's department, and mounting guard over the motor-car which had brought Madame Goldberg and which she had hired on the Place de l'Opéra in Paris.

The wife of the Antwerp diamond-merchant was stretched out on an iron bedstead on the first floor. A sheet had been thrown over her corpse which the doctor, that night, had half unclothed.

A fine April day was beginning. In the very field in which Maigret, dazzled by the headlamps, had vainly pursued the murderer, and in which he was now advancing step by step, following the traces left during the night, two peasants were loading beetroot from a hillock into a cart while the horses waited quietly.

The double line of trees along the main road barred the horizon. The garage's red petrol-pumps were sparkling in the sunshine.

Maigret was smoking as he walked along, slow, stubborn, perhaps disgruntled. The footprints found in the field seemed to show that Madame Goldberg had been killed by a rifle bullet, for the murderer had not come closer than thirty yards from the inn.

They were very ordinary footprints, of smooth-soled shoes

of average size. The trail went in a circle, ending up at the Three Widows Crossroads at about an equal distance from the Andersens' house, the Michonnets' villa, and the garage.

In short, it proved nothing. It provided no new lead, and Maigret, when he came out on to the road, was biting hard on the stem of his pipe.

He saw Monsieur Oscar at his door, his hands in the pockets of a pair of baggy trousers, and a self-satisfied expression on his common face.

'Up already, Chief-Inspector?' he shouted across the road.

At the same moment a motor-car stopped between the garage and Maigret. It was Andersen's little five-horse-power motor.

The Dane was at the wheel, gloves on his hands, a soft hat on his head, a cigarette between his lips. He raised his hat.

'Could I have a word with you, Chief-Inspector?'

After lowering the window, he went on with his habitual politeness:

'I wanted to ask your permission to go to Paris . . . I was hoping to meet you here . . . I'll tell you what takes me to Paris . . . Today's the 15th of April . . . It's today that I collect the money for my work at Dumas's . . . It's also today that I have to pay the rent . . .'

He gave an apologetic smile.

'Paltry errands, as you can see, but urgent errands for all that . . . I'm running short of money . . .'

He removed his black monocle for a moment in order to screw it in more firmly, and Maigret turned his head away, for he disliked meeting the fixed gaze of his glass eye.

'And your sister?'

'Precisely . . . I was going to speak to you about her . . . Would it be asking too much of you to get somebody to keep an eye on the house?'

Three dark motor-cars drove up the hill from Arpajon and turned left towards Avrainville.

'What's happening?'

'It's the Public Prosecutor's men ... Madame Goldberg was killed last night, just as she was getting out of a motor outside the inn ...'

Maigret watched for his reaction. On the other side of the road, Monsieur Oscar was idly sauntering up and down outside his garage.

'Killed!' repeated Carl.

And with a sudden nervousness he went on:

'Listen, Chief-Inspector! ... I really must go to Paris ... I can't stay here without any money, especially on the day the tradesmen present their bills ... But as soon as I get back I want to help find the murderer ... You will allow me to help, won't you? ... I don't know anything definite ... But I can feel ... how shall I put it? ... I can sense a plot of some sort.'

He had to draw in closer to the pavement, because a lorry returning from Paris was sounding its horn to ask him to make room.

'Off you go!' Maigret said to him.

Carl raised his hat again, and lit a cigarette before letting in the clutch. The old motor-car went down the hill and slowly climbed the opposite slope.

Three motors were standing at the entrance into Avrainville and silhouettes were moving about.

'Won't you have a drop of something?'

Maigret frowned as he looked at the smiling garage-proprietor, who was so persistent in offering him a drink.

Filling a pipe, he set off towards the house of the Three Widows, whose tall trees were full of the fluttering and twittering of birds. He had to pass the Michonnets' villa.

The windows were open. In the bedroom on the first floor

Madame Michonnet could be seen with a dust-cap on her head, busy shaking a rug.

On the ground floor the insurance agent, collarless, unshaven, tousle-haired, was looking at the road with an expression at once mournful and distant. He was smoking a meerschaum pipe with a cherrywood stem. When he caught sight of the Chief-Inspector, he pretended to be very busy knocking out his pipe and he studiously avoided greeting him.

A few moments later Maigret was ringing the bell at the gate of the Andersens' house. He waited in vain for ten minutes. All the shutters were closed. There was no sound to be heard, apart from the continuous chirping of the birds which were turning every tree into a world seething with life.

Finally he shrugged his shoulders, examined the lock, and picked a pass-key which opened it. And, as on the previous day, he went round the building to the french windows of the drawing-room.

He knocked on them and again obtained no reply. Then he went in, stubborn and peevish, throwing a glance at the gramophone, which was open, with a record on the turntable.

Why did it make him turn round? He would have been hard put to it to say. The needle grated. An Argentine orchestra played a tango as the Chief-Inspector started climbing the stairs.

On the first floor, Andersen's bedroom was open. Next to a hanging-wardrobe Maigret noticed a pair of shoes which had presumably just been cleaned, for the brush and tin of shoe-polish were still beside them, while the floor was strewn with powdered mud.

The Chief-Inspector had traced on a piece of paper the shape of the footprints found in the field. He compared footprints and shoes. They matched exactly.

And yet he did not give a start. He did not look pleased. He was still smoking, as disgruntled as when he had woken up.

A woman's voice called out.

'Is that you?'

He did not reply straight away. He could not see the woman who was speaking. The voice came from Else's room, the door of which was closed.

'It's me,' he said at last, speaking as indistinctly as possible.

A fairly long silence: then all of a sudden:

'Who's there?'

It was too late to pretend.

'The Chief-Inspector who was here yesterday. I should like to have a word with you, Mademoiselle . . .'

Another silence. Maigret tried to guess what she could be doing on the other side of the door, under which a thin line of light was showing.

'I'm listening,' she said at last.

'Perhaps you would be good enough to open the door? If you are not dressed, I can always wait . . .'

Always these irritating silences. A little laugh.

'You're asking me to do something very difficult, Chief-Inspector!'

'Why?'

'Because I'm locked in . . . So you'll have to talk to me without seeing me . . .'

'Who has locked you in?'

'My brother Carl . . . It's I who ask him to when he goes out, I'm so afraid of prowlers . . .'

Maigret said nothing but took his pass-key out of his pocket and quietly slipped it into the keyhole. His mouth was a little dry. Perhaps disturbing thoughts were passing through his mind?

When the key turned in the lock, he did not immediately push open the door but preferred to announce:

'I'm going to come in Mademoiselle . . .'

A strange impression. He was in a sunless corridor with dull walls, and suddenly he entered a place of light.

The Venetian shutters were closed. But the horizontal slats were letting in broad bands of sunlight.

The result was that the whole room was a jigsaw puzzle of light and shade. The walls, the objects, Else's face itself were so to speak cut up into luminous slices.

Added to that there was the young woman's cloying perfume and other vague details, silk underwear thrown on to an easy-chair, a Turkish cigarette smouldering in a porcelain bowl on a lacquered table, and finally Else, in a garnet-red dressing-gown, stretched out on the black velvet divan.

She looked at Maigret coming towards her with, in her wide-open eyes, an amused astonishment, mingled perhaps with a hint of fright.

'What are you doing?'

'I wanted to talk to you. Forgive me if I'm disturbing you.'

She laughed, a gay, mischievous laugh. One of her shoulders emerged from the dressing-gown, which she hitched up. And she remained recumbent, or rather curled up on the low divan which, like the entire room, was striped with sunshine.

'You see . . . I wasn't doing much . . . I never do anything!'

'Why didn't you go to Paris with your brother?'

'He doesn't want me to. He says that it's embarrassing having a woman around when men are talking business . . .'

'You never leave the house?'

'Oh yes! To go for walks in the park.'

'Just for that?'

'It's eight acres . . . That's enough for stretching my legs, isn't it? . . . But do sit down, Chief-Inspector . . . It's funny seeing you here on the sly . . .'

'What do you mean?'

'I mean that my brother will be furious when he gets back . . . He's worse than a mother, or a jealous lover! . . . It's he

46

who looks after me, and as you can see he takes his responsibilities seriously . . .'

'I thought it was you who wanted to be locked up, for fear of burglars . . .'

'That enters into it too . . . I've become so used to being on my own that I've ended up by being frightened of people . . .'

Maigret had sat down in an easy chair and had placed his bowler hat on the carpet. And every time that Else looked at him he turned his head away, because he could not accustom himself to that gaze of hers.

The day before, she had struck him as merely mysterious. In the half-light in which he had seen her, an almost hieratic figure, she had looked like a heroine of the screen and their encounter had retained a theatrical character.

Now he wanted to discover the woman's human side, but there was something else hindering him, and that was the very intimacy of the circumstances of their conversation.

The scented bedroom, with her lying there in her dressing-gown, dangling a slipper from the end of one bare foot, and a middle-aged, rather red-faced Maigret with his bowler hat on the floor, looked like a drawing in *La Vie Parisienne* . . .

He rather clumsily put his pipe in his pocket, although he had not emptied it.

'So you are bored here?'

'No . . . Yes . . . I don't know . . . Would you like a cigarette?'

She gestured towards a packet of Turkish cigarettes which was marked with the price 20 fr. 95, and Maigret recalled that the couple lived on two thousand francs a month, that Carl had to go and collect some money an hour before paying his rent and settling his tradesmen's bills.

'Do you smoke a lot?'

'One or two packets a day . . .'

She held out a finely chased cigarette-lighter, and heaved a sigh which opened her dressing-gown to reveal her breasts.

But the Chief-Inspector refrained from passing hasty judgement on her. In the society which haunts the luxury hotels he had seen extravagantly dressed foreigners whom a little clerk would have taken for prostitutes.

'Did your brother go out last night?'

'Do you think so?... I don't know...'

'You didn't spend the evening arguing with him?'

She showed her splendid teeth in a smile.

'Who told you that?... Was it he?... We argue sometimes, but in a nice way... Why, yesterday, for instance, I scolded him for not receiving you properly... He's so unsociable!... Even when he was very young...'

'You lived in Denmark?'

'Yes... In a big castle on the shores of the Baltic... A terribly gloomy castle, all white in a grey-green landscape... Do you know the country?... It's sinister... And yet it's beautiful too...'

Her eyes took on a nostalgic look. Her body quivered with pleasure.

'We were rich... But our parents were very strict, like most Protestants... For my part, I have no use for religion... But Carl is still a believer... Though rather less of a believer than his father, who lost the whole of his fortune because he clung to his scruples... Carl and I left the country...'

'Three years ago?'

'Yes... Just think of it: my brother was destined to become an important Court official... And instead he's forced to earn his living designing horrible fabrics... In Paris, in the second-class and even third-class hotels in which we had to stay, he was terribly unhappy... As a boy he had the same tutor as the Crown Prince... He preferred to bury himself here...'

'And bury you at the same time.'

'Yes . . . I'm used to it . . . In my parents' castle I was a prisoner too . . . All the girls who could have become friends of mine were kept away from me on the excuse that they weren't sufficiently high-born . . .'

Her facial expression changed with curious suddenness.

'Do you think,' she asked, 'that Carl has really become . . . . how shall I put it ? . . . abnormal ?'

And she bent forward as if to obtain the Chief-Inspector's opinion sooner.

'Are you afraid of that ?' asked Maigret in surprise.

'I didn't say that! I didn't say anything! Forgive me . . . You make me talk . . . I don't know why I've got such confidence in you . . . So . . .'

'He acts strangely sometimes ?'

She shrugged her shoulders wearily, crossed her legs, uncrossed them, and stood up, showing a brief glimpse of flesh between the flaps of her dressing-gown.

'What do you expect me to say to you ? . . . I don't know now . . . Since that business of the motor . . . Why should he have killed a man he doesn't know ?'

'You are sure you have never seen Isaac Goldberg before ?'

'Yes . . . As far as I know . . .'

'The two of you have never been to Antwerp ?'

'We stopped there for one night, on our way from Copenhagen three years ago . . . But no! My brother isn't capable of a thing like that . . . If he's become a little odd, I'm sure it's due much more to his accident than to our financial ruin . . . He was a handsome man . . . He still is when he's wearing his monocle . . . But otherwise, well . . . Can you see him kissing a woman without that piece of black glass ? . . . That dead eye surrounded by reddish flesh . . .'

She shuddered.

'That must be the main reason why he hides away . . .'

'But he's hiding you away too, by the same token!'

'What does that matter?'

'You're being sacrificed . . .'

'That's the fate of every woman, especially a sister . . . Things aren't quite the same in France . . . In our country, as in England, it's only the eldest son in a family, the heir to the name, who counts . . .'

She was getting on edge. She was drawing more jerkily and more deeply on her cigarette. She walked up and down, with the faint rays of light falling on her.

'No! Carl couldn't have committed that murder . . . There must have been a mistake . . . It's because you realized that that you let him go, isn't it . . .? Unless . . .'

'Unless?'

'Oh, this is something you wouldn't admit! I know that, for want of sufficient proof, the police sometimes let a suspect go, just so as to be able to trap him more surely later on . . . That would be odious of you! . . .'

She stubbed out her cigarette in the porcelain bowl.

'If only we hadn't picked on this sinister crossroads . . . Poor Carl, who was looking for solitude! . . . But we are less on our own here, Chief-Inspector, than in the most crowded district in Paris! . . . Across the way, there are those impossible, ridiculous people spying us . . . Especially the woman, with her white dustcap in the morning and her bun on one side in the afternoon . . . Then that garage, a little farther away . . . Three groups, three camps I'd say, at an equal distance from one another . . .'

'Used you to have any contact with the Michonnets?'

'No! The man came here once, about an insurance policy. Carl showed him the door . . .'

'And the proprietor of the garage?'

'He has never set foot here . . .'

'Was it your brother who wanted to run for it, on Sunday morning?'

She was silent for a while, her head bowed, a flush colouring her cheeks.

'No,' she sighed at last in a barely audible voice.

'It was you?'

'It was me . . . I hadn't thought about it then. I was nearly crazy at the idea that Carl could have committed a crime . . . The day before, I had seen him looking worried . . . So I carried him off . . .'

'He didn't swear to you that he was innocent?'

'Yes . . .'

'You didn't believe him?'

'Not straight away.'

'And now?'

She took her time in replying, pronouncing every syllable distinctly.

'I believe that, in spite of all his misfortunes, Carl is incapable of deliberately committing an evil deed . . . But listen, Chief-Inspector . . . He'll probably be coming back before long . . . If he finds you here, heaven knows what he'll think . . .'

She gave a smile in which, in spite of everything, there was a certain coquetry, if not indeed a hint of archness.

'You will defend him, won't you? . . . You'll get him out of this mess? . . . I should be so grateful to you!'

She held out her hand to him and, with this gesture, the dressing-gown opened again.

'Good-bye, Chief-Inspector . . .'

He picked up his hat and edged his way out of the room.

'Can you lock the door again, so that he doesn't notice anything?'

A few moments later Maigret was going downstairs, crossing the drawing-room with the heterogeneous furniture, and walking out on to the terrace which was already flooded with warm sunshine.

Motor-cars were humming along the road. The gate did not creak while he was shutting it.

As he was passing the garage, a mocking voice called out: 'Well, you're not easily scared, are you?'

It was Monsieur Oscar, vulgar and jovial. He added:

'Come on, now! Come in and have a drink! Those chaps from the Public Prosecutor's office have already gone. You must have a minute to spare!'

The Chief-Inspector hesitated, wincing as a mechanic grated his file on a piece of steel held in a vice.

'Ten litres!' shouted a motorist who had drawn up beside one of the pumps. 'Isn't there anybody there?'

Monsieur Michonnet, who was unshaven and had not put on a collar, was standing in his tiny garden, looking at the road over the railing.

'At last!' exclaimed Monsieur Oscar, seeing Maigret preparing to follow him. 'I like people who don't give themselves airs. Not like that stuck-up fellow at the Three Widows!...'

CHAPTER 5

The Abandoned Motor

'THIS way, Chief-Inspector! . . . It isn't very luxurious, mind you . . . We're just ordinary working folk . . .'

He pushed open the door of the house behind the garage and then went straight into a kitchen which obviously served as a dining-room, for there were still breakfast things on the table.

A woman in a pink crepon dressing-gown broke off polishing a brass tap.

'Come here, ducks, and let me introduce Chief-Inspector Maigret . . . My wife, Chief-Inspector . . . Mind you, she could have a maid if she wanted to . . . But she'd have nothing left to do and she'd get bored . . .'

She was neither ugly nor pretty. She was about thirty. Her dressing-gown was vulgar and unattractive, and she stood awkwardly in front of Maigret, looking at her husband.

'Go on, give us an apéritif! . . . A blackcurrant liqueur, Chief-Inspector? . . . You want to go into the drawing-room? . . . No? . . . So much the better! . . . I'm an easy-going sort of chap . . . That's right, isn't it ducks? . . . No, not those glasses! . . . A couple of big glasses!'

He leant back in his chair. He was wearing a pink shirt, without a waistcoat, and he slipped his hands inside his belt, over his portly stomach.

'Exciting, isn't she, the little lady at the Three Widows? . . . Can't say in front of my wife, of course . . . But between ourselves, she's quite a titbit for any man . . . The trouble is, there's that brother of hers . . . Or so he calls himself . . . A miserable-looking chap who spends his time spying on her

... They even say around here that when he goes out for an hour he locks her up, and that he does the same thing every night ... You think that sounds like a brother and sister? .. Bottoms up! ... Look here, ducks, go and tell Jojo not to forget to repair that Lardy chap's lorry ...'

Maigret glanced towards the window, because he heard the sound of an engine which reminded him of the noise of a five-horse-power motor-car.

'No, that isn't it, Chief-Inspector! ... I can tell you, with my eyes shut, from here, exactly what is going past along the road ... That old crock belongs to the engineer at the power-house ... You're waiting for our lord of the manor to come back?'

The hands of an alarm-clock on a shelf stood at eleven o'clock. Through an open door Maigret saw a corridor in which there was a wall-telephone.

'You aren't drinking ... Here's to your investigations! ... It's a rum business, don't you think? .... The idea of switching the motors, and above all of pinching the six-cylinder from the old fossil across the road! ... Because he's an old fossil all right! ... Oh, we've got some wonderful neighbours, I can tell you that! It has been fun watching you coming and going since you got here yesterday ... And above all seeing you looking at people as if you suspected them all ... Mind you, I've got a cousin on my wife's side who was in the police ... The Gambling Squad ... He was at the races every afternoon, and the funniest thing of all was that he used to pass tips on to me ... Bottoms up! Well, ducks, have you finished?'

'Yes ...'

The young woman, who had just come in again, stood there for a moment wondering what to do.

'Come on, now, have a drink with us ... The Chief-Inspector isn't a snob, and he isn't going to refuse to drink your health just because you've got your hair in curlers ...'

'Do you mind if I make a phone-call?' asked Maigret.

'Go ahead! Turn the handle ... If it's for Paris, they'll put you through straight away.'

First of all he looked in the directory for the number of Dumas et Fils, the manufacturers at whose office Carl Andersen was supposed to be collecting some money.

The conversation was a brief one. The cashier, whom he had at the end of the line, confirmed that Andersen had two thousand francs due to him that day, but added that so far he had not been seen in the rue du Quatre-Septembre.

When Maigret came back into the kitchen, Monsieur Oscar was ostentatiously rubbing his hands.

'You know, I must say that I'm enjoying this ... Because I know the ropes, of course. Something happens at the crossroads ... There are only three sets of people living here ... Naturally you suspect all three ... Yes, you do! Don't play the innocent ... I saw straight away that you didn't trust me and that you weren't keen on having a drink with me ... Three houses ... The insurance agent looks too stupid to be capable of committing a crime ... The lord of the manor is a real gent ... So there's nobody left but yours truly, a poor devil of a workman who's managed to become his own boss but doesn't know how to behave in polite society ... A former boxer! ... If you ask them about me at the Police Headquarters, they'll tell you that I've been picked up two or three times in raids, because I used to enjoy going to the rue de Lappe to dance a java, especially in the days when I was a boxer ... Another time I gave a poke in the kisser to a copper who was annoying me ... Bottoms up, Chief-Inspector!'

'No, thanks.'

'You aren't going to refuse! A blackcurrant liqueur never hurt anybody ... You know, I like to put my cards on the table ... It got on my nerves seeing you snooping round my garage and looking at me on the sly ... That's right isn't it, ducks? Didn't I say as much to you last night? ... The Chief-Inspector's there! Well, let him come in! Let him rummage around all over the place! ... Let him search me! And then he'll have to admit that I'm a good chap as honest as the day is long ... What fascinates me about this story is the motors ... Because when all's said and done, it's all a matter of motors ...'

Half past eleven. Maigret stood up.

'Another phone-call I've got to make ...'

Wearing a worried frown, he asked for Police Headquarters, and told an inspector to send a description of Andersen's five-horse-power motor to all police-stations, as well as to the frontier-posts.

Monsieur Oscar had drunk four apéritifs and his cheeks were pinker as a result, his eyes bright.

'I know you'll refuse to have a *blanquette de veau* with us ... Especially seeing that here we eat in the kitchen ... Never mind! There's Groslumeau's lorry coming back from the Central Market ... Excuse me, Chief-Inspector ...'

He went out. Maigret was left alone with the young woman, who was stirring a saucepan with a wooden spoon.

'You've got a gay husband!'

'Yes ... He's very jolly ...'

'And brutal at times, eh?'

'He doesn't like being contradicted ... But he's a good sort ...'

'Rather an eye for the girls?'

She made no reply.

'I bet he goes on the binge now and then ...'

'Like all men ...'

Her voice turned bitter. Snatches of conversation could be heard from the direction of the garage.

'Put it down there! ... Right ... Yes ... We'll change your back tyres tomorrow morning ...'

Monsieur Oscar came back in high spirits. You could tell that he felt like singing and playing the fool.

'You're sure you won't have a bite with us, Chief-Inspector ... We could have a bottle of wine from the cellar ... What are you pulling a face like that for, Germaine? ... Oh, women! ... They can never stay in the same mood two hours running ...'

'I've got to go back to Avrainville,' said Maigret.

'Can I drive you over there? ... It won't take a minute.'

'No, thank you. I'd rather walk.'

Outside, Maigret plunged into an atmosphere warm with sunshine, and on the road to Avrainville he was preceded by a yellow butterfly.

A hundred yards from the inn he met Sergeant Lucas coming to meet him.

'Well?'

'Just as you thought ... The doctor has taken out the bullet ... It's a rifle bullet ...'

'Nothing else?'

'Yes. We've some information from Paris ... Isaac Goldberg arrived there in his motor, a Minerva sports model in which he normally travelled about and which he drove himself ... It was in that motor that he must have done the journey from Paris to the crossroads.'

'Is that all?'

'We're waiting for information from the Belgian Police.'

The limousine from which Madame Goldberg had been alighting when she had been killed had gone off with its driver.

'And the body?'

'They've taken it to Arpajon ... The examining magistrate is worried ... He asked me to tell you to hurry ... What he's particularly scared of is that the Brussels and Antwerp papers will give too much publicity to the case ...'

Maigret started humming to himself, went into the inn, and sat down at his table.

'Is there a telephone here?'

'Yes. But it doesn't work between midday and two o'clock. It's half past twelve.'

The Chief-Inspector ate in silence and Lucas gathered that he was preoccupied. Several times the Sergeant tried in vain to start a conversation.

It was one of the first fine days of spring. When the meal was over, Maigret dragged his chair into the yard, placed it next to a wall, in the midst of the hens and ducks, and dozed in the sunshine for half an hour.

But on the stroke of two o'clock he was on his feet, unhooking the telephone.

'Hullo . . . Police Headquarters? They still haven't found Andersen's motor?'

He started walking round and round the courtyard. Ten minutes later he was called back to the telephone. It was the Quai des Orfèvres.

'Chief-Inspector Maigret . . . We've just had a phone-call from Jeumont . . . The motor's there . . . It's been abandoned opposite the station . . . I suppose the driver preferred to cross the frontier on foot or by train . . .'

Maigret replaced the receiver for only a moment, then asked for the firm of Dumas et Fils. They told him that Carl Andersen had still not called to collect his two thousand francs.

*

When, about three o'clock, Maigret, with Lucas by his side, passed the garage, Monsieur Oscar appeared from behind a motor-car and gaily asked:

'How are things, Chief-Inspector?'

Maigret gave only a wave in reply and continued on his way to the house of the Three Widows.

The doors and windows of the Michonnets' villa were shut, but, once again, a curtain quivered in the dining-room window.

It was as if the garage-proprietor's good humour had yet again annoyed the Chief-Inspector, who was drawing furiously on his pipe.

'The fact that Andersen has run for it . . .,' began Lucas in a conciliatory tone of voice.

'Stay here!'

As he had done that morning, he went into the park of the house of the Three Widows first, then into the house itself. In the drawing-room he sniffed, looked carefully around him, and made out the trails of smoke in the corners of the room.

And there was a smell of tobacco hanging around which had not gone stale.

It was instinctive. He put his hand over the butt of his revolver before starting to climb the stairs. On the way he heard the music of a gramophone, and recognized the tango it had been playing in the morning.

The sound was coming from Else's bedroom. When he knocked, the gramophone stopped short.

'Who's there?'

'The Chief-Inspector . . .'

A short laugh.

'In that case, you know what to do to get in . . . I can't open the door to you . . .'

The pass-key worked once more. The young woman was dressed. She was wearing the same close-fitting black dress as the day before.

'It is you who have prevented my brother from coming home?'

'No, I haven't seen him since this morning.'

'Then his account at Dumas's probably wasn't ready. He sometimes has to go back in the afternoon . . .'

59

'Your brother has tried to cross the Belgian frontier. Everything suggests that he has succeeded.'

She looked at him with an expression of amazement not unmixed with incredulity.

'Carl?'

'Yes.'

'You're testing me, aren't you?'

'Can you drive?'

'Drive what?'

'A motor-car.'

'No. My brother has always refused to teach me.'

Maigret had not taken his pipe out of his mouth. He was still wearing his hat.

'Have you been out of this room?'

'Me?'

She laughed. An innocent, tinkling laugh, more than ever endowed with what Americans call sex-appeal.

For a woman can be beautiful without being attractive. Others, with less regular features, unfailingly arouse either desire or a sentimental nostalgia.

Else inspired both. She was at once woman and child. The atmosphere around her had a sensual charm. And yet, when she looked somebody in the face, one was surprised to see that she had the limpid eyes of a little girl.

'I don't know what you mean.'

'Somebody smoked a cigarette, less than half an hour ago, in the drawing-room downstairs.'

'Who?'

'That's what I'm asking you.'

'And how do you expect me to know?'

'The gramophone was downstairs this morning.'

'Impossible! ... How do you expect ... I say! ... Chief-Inspector! ... I hope you don't suspect me? ... You've got a peculiar look in your eyes ... Where is Carl?'

60

'I tell you he's crossed the frontier.'

'That isn't true! It's impossible! Why would he have done that? . . . Not to mention the fact that he wouldn't have left me here alone. Why, the very idea! What would become of me, with nobody to look after me?'

It was baffling. Without warning, without any extravagant gestures, without raising her voice, she achieved a pathetic effect. It came from her eyes. An indescribable agitation. An expression of anxiety, of supplication.

'Tell me the truth, Chief-Inspector! . . . Carl isn't guilty, is he? . . . If he was, it would mean he'd gone mad! . . . I refuse to believe it! It frightens me . . . In his family . . .'

'There are cases of insanity?'

She turned her head away.

'Yes . . . His grandfather . . . He died of an attack of insanity . . . One of his aunts is in an asylum . . . But not him! . . . No! . . . I know him . . .'

'Have you had lunch?'

She gave a start, looked around her, and replied in surprise: 'No.'

'And you aren't hungry? . . . It's three o'clock.'

'Yes, I do feel hungry.'

'Then go and have lunch. There's no longer any reason why you should stay locked up. Your brother won't come back . . .'

'That isn't true! He'll come back! He can't leave me on my own.'

'Come along.'

Maigret was already in the corridor. He was frowning. He was still smoking. He did not take his eyes off the girl.

She brushed against him as she passed but he remained unaffected. Downstairs she seemed even more at a loss.

'It was always Carl who served me. I don't even know if there's anything to eat . . .'

There was at least a tin of condensed milk and a loaf of fancy bread in the kitchen.

'I can't . . . I'm too strung up . . . Leave me alone . . . Or rather, no, don't leave me! . . . This horrible house that I've never liked . . . What's that out there?'

Through the french window she pointed to an animal curled up in a ball on one of the paths in the park. An ordinary cat.

'I hate animals! I hate the country! It's full of creaking noises that make me jump . . . At night, every night, there's an owl somewhere that hoots horribly . . .'

Doors presumably frightened her too, for she looked at them as if she expected to see enemies appearing on all sides.

'I can't sleep here alone! . . . I won't!'

'Is there a telephone?'

'No . . . My brother thought of having one installed . . . But it's too dear for us . . . Just think of it! . . . Living in a house as big as this, with a park of heaven knows how many acres, and not being able to afford a telephone, or electricity, or even a charwoman to do the heavy work! . . . That's Carl all over! . . . Just like his father!'

And suddenly she started laughing hysterically.

It was embarrassing, for she could not manage to regain her composure, and in the end, while her body was still shaking with laughter, her eyes were full of anxiety.

'What's the matter? What's so funny?'

'Nothing. You musn't take any notice. I was thinking of our childhood, of Carl's tutor, of our castle in Denmark, with all the servants, the visitors, the carriages drawn by four horses . . . And here . . .'

She knocked over the tin of milk, and went and pressed her forehead against the glass of the french window, staring at the sun-baked steps.

'I'll arrange for a policeman to keep an eye on you tonight.'

'Yes, please ... No, I don't want a policeman ... I want you to come here yourself, Chief-Inspector ... Otherwise I'll be frightened ...'

Was she laughing or crying? She was breathing hard. Her whole body was shaking from head to foot.

One might have thought that she was poking fun at somebody. But one might also have thought that she was on the verge of an attack of hysterics.

'Don't leave me alone.'

'I've got my work to do.'

'But seeing that Carl has run away!'

'You think he's guilty?'

'I don't know! I don't know any more! If he's run away ...'

'Do you want me to lock you up in your room again?'

'No! What I want to do, as soon as possible, tomorrow morning, is to get away from this house, away from this crossroads ... I want to go to Paris, where the streets are full of people, full of life ... The country frightens me ... I don't know ...'

And all of a sudden:

'Will they arrest Carl in Belgium?'

'A warrant will be issued for his extradition.'

'It's incredible ... When I think that only three days ago ...'

She took her head in both hands and ruffled her fair hair.

Maigret was on the steps.

'See you later, Mademoiselle.'

He went away with a sense of relief and yet he was sorry to leave her. Lucas was walking up and down the road.

'No news?'

'Not a thing! ... The insurance agent came and asked me if he was going to be given a new motor soon.'

Monsieur Michonnet had preferred to ask Lucas rather than

63

Maigret. And he could be seen in his little garden, watching the two men.

'So he's got nothing to do?'

'He says he can't visit his clients in the country without a motor ... He talks about suing us for damages ...'

A van and a tourer containing a whole family were standing in front of the petrol-pumps.

'One chap's got plenty to do,' said the sergeant. 'And that's the garage proprietor! ... It seems he earns as much as he likes ... Busy night and day, that place is ...'

'Have you any tobacco?'

The unaccustomed sunshine blazing down on to the countryside was surprising and oppressive, and Maigret mopped his brow, murmuring:

'I'm going to have a nap for an hour ... Tonight we'll see what we can do ...'

As he was passing the garage Monsieur Oscar called out to him:

'A drop of rot-gut, Chief Inspector? Just to wet your whistle ...'

'Another time!'

The sound of raised voices suggested that in the millstone villa Monsieur Michonnet was quarrelling with his wife.

CHAPTER 6

The Night of the Missing Persons

IT was five o'clock in the afternoon when Maigret was woken up by Lucas, who had brought him a telegram from the Belgian police.

Isaac Goldberg had been watched for several months because scale of business did not correspond to standard of living. Stop. Was particularly suspected of trafficking in stolen jewels. Stop. No proof. Stop. Journey to France coincided with theft of jewels worth two million in London a fortnight ago. Stop. Anonymous letter stated jewels were at Antwerp. Stop. Two international thieves have been seen there spending freely. Stop. Believe Goldberg bought jewels and went to France to dispose of them. Stop. Asking Scotland Yard for description of jewels.

Maigret, still half-asleep, stuffed the paper into his pocket and asked:

'Nothing else?'

'No, I've gone on watching the crossroads. I saw the garage-proprietor in his Sunday best and asked him where he was going. It seems he's in the habit of taking his wife out to dinner in Paris once a week and afterwards going to the theatre. When that happens he only comes back the next day, because he spends the night in a hotel.'

'Has he gone?'

'Yes, he must have gone by now.'

'Did you ask him where he has dinner?'

'At the Escargot in the rue de la Bastille. Then he goes to the Ambigu Theatre. He puts up at the Hôtel Rambuteau in the rue de Rivoli.'

'All cut and dried!' grunted Maigret, running a comb through his hair.

'The insurance agent told me through his wife that he'd like to talk to you, or rather to have a chat with you, to use his own words.'

'Is that all?'

Maigret went into the kitchen, where the innkeeper's wife was cooking the evening meal. He took a pot of *pâté*, cut himself a thick chunk of bread, and ordered:

'A mug of white wine, please.'

'You aren't going to wait for dinner?'

He ate his huge sandwich without answering.

The sergeant watched him with an obvious longing to speak.

'You expect something important to happen tonight, don't you?'

'Hmm . . .'

But why deny it? Didn't this meal he was having standing up suggest the eve of battle?

'I thought it all over just now. I tried to sort out my ideas. It isn't easy . . .'

Maigret looked at him quietly, his jaws working all the time.

'It's still the girl that puzzles me most of all. Sometimes I think that all the people round her – the garage-proprietor, the insurance agent, the Dane – are guilty, but not her. Sometimes I feel like swearing the very opposite, that she's the only poisonous element here . . .'

There was a gleam of amusement in the eyes of the Chief-Inspector, who seemed to be saying:

'Go on!'

'There are moments when she really looks like a girl of good family . . . But there are others when she reminds me of the time I spent in the Vice Squad . . . You know what I mean

66

... The sort of girl who, with the coolest cheek in the world, tells you some cock-and-bull story. But the details are so odd that it seems she can't possibly have invented them ... You fall for the story ... Then, under her pillow, you find an old novelette and you realize that it's there that she got all the material for her tale ... The sort of woman who tells a lie with every breath she draws and perhaps even ends up by believing what she says!'

'Is that all?'

'You think I'm wrong?'

'I honestly don't know.'

'Mind you, I don't always think the same thing, and more often it's Andersen that worries me ... Just imagine a man like him, well-bred, educated, intelligent, putting himself at the head of a gang ...'

'We'll see him tonight!'

'Him! ... But if he's crossed the frontier ...'

'Hmm!'

'You think that ...'

'That the whole business is ten times more complicated than you imagine ... And that it's better not to puzzle over everything but to stick to a few important elements.

'For instance, the fact that it was Monsieur Michonnet who was the first to lodge a complaint and that he has asked me to go to his house tonight ...

'The very night when the garage-proprietor is in Paris ... *Very ostentatiously*! ...

'Goldberg's Minerva has disappeared. Remember that too. And seeing that there aren't many Minervas in France, it's no easy matter making it vanish into thin air ...'

'You think that Monsieur Oscar? ...'

'Not so fast! Just play about with those three facts, if it amuses you.'

'But Else?'

'What, again?'

And Maigret, wiping his mouth, went out on to the road. A quarter of an hour later he was ringing the bell at the Michonnets' villa, and it was the wife's sour face which greeted him.

'My husband's waiting for you up there.'

'That's too kind of him ...'

She did not notice the irony in these words and went upstairs in front of the Chief-Inspector. Monsieur Michonnet was in his bedroom, close to the window, whose blind he had pulled down. He was sitting in a Voltaire armchair with a tartan rug round his legs, and it was in an aggressive voice that he asked:

'Well, when am I going to get another car? ... You think it's smart of you, I suppose, to take the bread and butter out of a man's mouth? ... And in the meantime you go and pay court to that woman across the road, or else have drinks with the garage proprietor! ... Oh, they're a fine lot, the police! I am not going to mince my words, Chief-Inspector. Yes, they're a fine lot! ... It doesn't matter about the murderer. It's much more important annoying ordinary decent folk ... I've got a motor-car ... Now is it mine or isn't it? ... That's what I want to know. Go on, tell me! ... Is it mine? ... Good. Then what right have you to keep it under lock and key? ...'

'Are you ill?' Maigret asked quietly, glancing at the blanket round the insurance agent's legs.

'Who wouldn't be in my position? This business has poisoned my system. And it's in the legs it always gets me ... An attack of gout! ... I can look forward to two or three nights in this armchair, without any sleep ... If I asked you to come here it was to tell you this: You can see what sort of condition I'm in! You can see that I'm incapable of doing any work, especially without a car! That's all ... I shall call you as a witness when I bring an action for damages . . . Good night to you, Monsieur!'

All this was recited with the exaggerated bluster of a man confident that he was in the right. Madame Michonnet added:

'Only while you prowl around looking as if you're spying on us, the murderer's still at large . . . There's justice for you . . . Attack the little man, but leave the big fellow alone.'

'Is that all you have to say to me?'

Monsieur Michonnet scowled and sank further into his armchair. His wife walked towards the door.

The inside of the house matched the front: suites of furniture, spotless, highly polished, and rooted to the floor as if they were never used.

In the corridor Maigret stopped in front of an old-fashioned telephone fastened to the wall. And in the presence of an outraged Madame Michonnet he turned the handle.

'This is the police, Mademoiselle. Could you tell me if there have been any calls this afternoon for the Three Widows Crossroads? . . . You say there are two numbers, the garage and the Michonnets' house? . . . Right . . . Well? . . . The garage had one call from Paris about one o'clock and another about five? . . . And the other number? . . . Just one call . . . From Paris? . . . Five past five? . . . Thank you . . .'

He looked at Madame Michonnet with eyes twinkling mischievously and gave a bow.

'I wish you a good night, Madame.'

He opened the gate of the house of the Three Widows with easy familiarity, walked round the building, and went up to the first floor.

Else Andersen, looking very agitated, came to meet him.

'I'm sorry to bother you like this, Chief-Inspector. You're going to think I'm presuming on you . . . But I'm all on edge

69

... I'm frightened, I don't know why ... Since our conversation earlier on, it seems to me that you're the only one who can protect me ... You know this sinister crossroads as well as I do now, these three houses which look as if they're challenging one another ... Do you believe in premonitions? ... I do, like all women ... I feel that something is going to happen tonight ...'

'And you're asking me again to keep an eye on you?'

'I'm asking too much of you, aren't I? ... But is it my fault if I'm frightened?'

Maigret's gaze had settled on a picture of a snow-covered landscape, which was hung awry. But the next moment the Chief-Inspector had turned towards the girl who was waiting for his answer.

'You're not afraid for your reputation?'

'What does that matter when one's frightened?'

'In that case I'll come back in an hour ... I've a few orders to give ...'

'Really and truly! ... You'll come back? ... You mean it? ... Besides, I've got a lot of things to tell you, things that have only come back to me bit by bit ...'

'What about?'

'About my brother ... But they're probably not important ... For instance, I remember that after his flying accident, the doctor who attended him told my father that he could answer for his physical health but not for his mental health ... I never thought about that remark before ... Some other details too ... This insistence on living out in the country, on hiding away ... I'll tell you all that when you come back ...'

And she smiled at him with a gratitude still mingled with a little fear.

*

As he passed the millstone villa, Maigret automatically glanced at the first-floor window, which shone out bright yellow in the darkness. On the illuminated blind there stood out the silhouette of Monsieur Michonnet sitting in his arm-chair.

At the inn the Chief-Inspector simply gave Lucas a few orders, without any explanation.

'Get half-a-dozen inspectors over here and post them round the crossroads. Every hour, make sure that Monsieur Oscar is still in Paris, by phoning the Escargot, the theatre, and the hotel. Have somebody following anybody who leaves one of the three houses . . .'

'Where will you be?'

'At the Andersens' house.'

'You think that . . .?'

'I don't think anything at all, old chap. See you soon, or else tomorrow morning.'

Night had fallen. On his way back to the main road, the Chief-Inspector checked the cartridge-clip of his revolver and made sure there was some tobacco in his pouch.

Behind the Michonnets' window the shadow of the arm-chair and the insurance agent's moustachioed profile could still be seen.

Else Andersen had exchanged her black velvet dress for the dressing-gown she had been wearing in the morning and Maigret found her stretched out on the divan, smoking a ciga-rette, calmer than she had been at their last meeting, but with her forehead furrowed in thought.

'If you only knew what a lot of good it does me to know you are here Chief-Inspector! . . . There are some people who inspire confidence at the first glance . . . They are rare birds! . . . For my part, in any case, I've met very few people I could trust instinctively . . . You may smoke . . .'

'Have you had dinner?'

'I'm not hungry . . . I can't think how I keep going . . . For the past four days, ever since that horrible discovery of the corpse in the motor, I've been thinking, thinking . . . I keep trying to arrive an opinion, to understand . . .'

'And you come to the conclusion that it's your brother who's guilty?'

'No . . . I don't want to accuse Carl . . . Especially seeing that, even if he were guilty in the strict sense of the word, it could only be because he had acted in a fit of madness . . . You've picked the worst armchair . . . If you'd like to lie down, there's a camp bed in the next room . . .'

She was calm and agitated at the same time. A calm which was external, deliberate, acquired with considerable difficulty. An agitation which at certain moments showed through in spite of everything.

'Something horrible has already happened in this house, hasn't it, a long time ago? . . . Carl has spoken to me about it, evasively . . . He's afraid of frightening me . . . He always treats me like a little girl . . .'

She bent forward, with a supple movement of the whole body, to drop the ash of her cigarette into the porcelain bowl on the little table. The dressing-gown opened, as it had done that morning. For a moment one small round breast was visible. It was only a glimpse, and yet Maigret had had time to make out a scar, the sight of which made him frown.

'You were wounded once?'

'What do you mean?'

She had blushed. She instinctively drew her dressing-gown together over her chest.

'You've got a scar on your right breast.'

She looked extremely embarrassed.

'Excuse me,' she said. 'Here I'm in the habit of living with very little on . . . I didn't think . . . As for that scar . . . You know, that's another thing I've suddenly remembered . . . But it must be a coincidence . . . When we were still children, Carl and I, we used to play in the castle park and I remember that once Carl was given a rifle for St Nicholas's Day ... He must have been fourteen ... It's silly, as you'll see for yourself ... To begin with, he fired at a target ... Then, the day after an evening at the circus, he decided to play at William Tell ... I held a target-card in each hand ... The first bullet hit me in the chest ...'

Maigret had got to his feet. He walked towards the divan, his face so inscrutable that she looked worried as she watched him approaching and her hands clutched hold of her dressing-gown.

But it was not at her that he was looking. He was gazing at the wall above the divan, where the picture of the snow-covered landscape was now hanging in an absolutely horizontal position.

With a slow gesture he pushed the frame to one side, revealing a hole in the wall, not a big or deep hole, but simply a niche where two bricks had been removed.

In this niche there was an automatic loaded with six bullets, a box of cartridges, a key, and a tube of veronal.

Else had followed his movements but showed scarcely any sign of emotion. A touch of pink in her cheeks. A little more brightness in her eyes.

'I would probably have shown you that hiding-place later on, Chief-Inspector ...'

'Really?'

As he spoke he thrust the revolver into his pocket, noted that half the veronal tablets in the tube were missing, and went over to the door to try the key in the lock, where it fitted perfectly.

The young woman had risen to her feet. She no longer bothered to cover her chest. She gestured jerkily with her hands while she spoke.

'What you've just found is confirmation of what I've already told you ... But you must try to understand me ... How could I accuse my brother?... If I had told you, the first time you came here, that for a long time I had thought he was mad, you would have been shocked... And yet that's the truth ...'

Her accent, which was stronger when she spoke excitedly, gave a strange quality to the least thing she said.

'And this revolver?'

'How can I explain?... When we left Denmark, we were ruined ... But my brother was convinced that with his culture he would find a splendid post in Paris ... He didn't succeed ... The result was that his moods became even more worrying ... When he decided to bury us here, I realized that he was seriously ill ... Especially when he insisted on locking me up every night under the pretext that enemies might attack us!... Just imagine my position here, between these four walls, with no hope of getting out in the event of a fire, for instance, or any other sort of accident ... I couldn't sleep ... I was as terrified as if I had been in an underground passage.

'One day when he was in Paris I sent for a locksmith who made me a key to my bedroom ... To do that, I had to climb out of the window as he had locked me in ...

'My freedom of movement was secured ... But that was not enough!... Carl had days of near-insanity; often he spoke of destroying us both rather than endure complete degeneration ...

'I bought a revolver at Arpajon, during another of my brother's trips to Paris ... And as I slept badly I got myself some veronal ...

'You see how simple it is!... He's very suspicious ... There's nothing more suspicious than a man whose mind is unbalanced but who is still clear-sighted enough to realize it ... At night I made this hiding-place ...'

'Is that all?'

She was surprised by the abruptness of this question.

74

'Don't you believe me?'

He made no reply, walked over to the window, opened it, pushed the shutters apart, and was bathed in the cool night air.

The road beneath him was like a trail of ink reflecting gleams of moonlight whenever a motor-car passed. The headlamps could be seen far away, perhaps at a distance of five or six miles. Then all of a sudden there was a sort of cyclone, a rush of air, a roaring noise, and a little red light disappearing into the distance.

The petrol-pumps were lit up. In the Michonnets' villa there was a solitary light, on the first floor, and the silhouette of the armchair and the insurance agent could still be seen against the blind.

'Close the window, Chief-Inspector!'

He turned and saw Else shivering, huddled up in her dressing-gown.

'Now can you understand why I'm worried? ... You've got me to tell you everything ... And yet I wouldn't want anything to happen to Carl, not for anything in the world ... He has often said to me that we should die together ...'

'Please be quiet!'

He was listening intently to the noises of the night. To do that, he drew his armchair up to the window and put his feet on the rail.

'But I tell you I'm cold ...'

'Put some more clothes on.'

'Don't you believe me?'

'Be quiet, dammit!'

And he started smoking. In the distance there were vague farm noises, a cow lowing, things moving about indistinctly. In the garage, on the other hand, steel objects were being knocked together, and then all of a sudden the electric motor used for blowing up tyres could be heard vibrating.

'But I trusted you . . . And now . . .'

'Will you be quiet or won't you?'

Behind a tree by the road, close to the house, he had made out a shadow which was presumably one of the inspectors he had asked for.

'I'm hungry . . .'

He swung round angrily to face the young woman, who was looking very sorry for herself.

'Go and get something to eat!'

'I daren't go downstairs . . . I'm frightened . . .'

He shrugged his shoulders, made sure that everything was quiet outside, and suddenly decided to go down to the ground floor. He knew his way round the kitchen. By the stove there was a little cold meat, some bread, and a half-empty bottle of beer.

He took all this upstairs and put it on the little table, next to the cigarette-bowl.

'You're being nasty to me, Chief-Inspector . . .'

She looked so much like a little girl. You could feel that she was on the point of bursting into tears.

'I haven't time to be either nice or nasty . . . Eat up!'

'Aren't you hungry? . . . Are you cross with me for telling you the truth?'

But he had already turned his back on her and was looking out of the window. Madame Michonnet, behind the blind, was bending over her husband, to whom she was probably giving some medicine, for she was holding a spoon towards his face.

Else had picked up a piece of meat with her fingers. She nibbled at it with obvious distaste. Then she poured herself a glass of beer.

'That was awful,' she declared, giving a shudder. 'But why don't you shut that window? . . . I'm frightened . . . Haven't you any heart?'

He shut it suddenly, angrily, and looked Else up and down as if he were going to lose his temper.

It was at that moment that he saw her turn pale, her blue eyes glazed over, and one hand stretched out for support. He just had time to rush over to her and put one arm round her waist as she doubled up.

He gently lowered her on to the floor, lifted her eyelids to examine her eyes, and picked up the empty beer glass. He sniffed this and found that it gave off a bitter smell.

There was a teaspoon on the table. He used it to force Else's teeth apart. Then, without hesitating, he plunged the spoon into her mouth and started tickling the back of the throat and the palate.

Her face twitched and spasms shook her chest.

Else was stretched out on the carpet. Tears were trickling from her eyelids. Just as her head was falling to one side, she gave a big hiccough.

Thanks to the contraction produced by the spoon, her stomach was loosened. A little pool of yellowish liquid stained the carpet and a few drops fell on her dressing-gown.

Maigret took the water-jug from the dressing-table and moistened her face all over.

He kept turning impatiently towards the window.

And she was taking a long time to come to. She groaned feebly. Finally she raised her head.

'What . . .?'

She stood up, bewildered, still unsteady on her feet, and saw the stained carpet, the spoon, the beer-glass.

Then she started sobbing, her head in her hands.

'You can see that I had reason to be frightened! . . . They've tried to poison me . . . And you wouldn't believe me! . . . You . . .'

She gave a start at the same time as Maigret. And both of them stayed motionless for a while, listening intently.

A shot had been fired close to the house, probably in the garden. It had been followed by a hoarse cry.

And then, from the direction of the road, came a long blast on a whistle. People were running. The gate was shaken. Through the window Maigret could see his inspectors' torches probing the darkness. And barely a hundred yards away, the Michonnets' window, and Madame Michonnet arranging a pillow behind her husband's head . . .

The Chief-Inspector opened the door. He heard a noise on the ground floor.

It was Lucas calling out:

'Chief!'

'Who is it?'

'Carl Andersen . . . He isn't dead . . . Are you coming?'

Maigret turned round and saw Else sitting on the edge of the divan, her elbows on her knees, her chin cupped in her hands, staring straight ahead, while her teeth were clenched and her body was shaking convulsively.

CHAPTER 7

The Two Wounds

CARL ANDERSEN was carried into his bedroom. An inspector followed, holding the lamp from downstairs. The wounded man did not groan, did not move. Only when he was stretched out on his bed did Maigret bend over him and note that his eyelids were half-open.

Andersen recognized him, looked less overcome, and reached out for the Chief-Inspector's hand, murmuring:

'Else?'

She was standing in the doorway, hollow-eyed, in an attitude of anxious expectation.

It was quite an impressive scene. Carl had lost his black monocle, and beside his sound eye which was bloodshot, half-closed, his glass eye retained its artificial fixity.

The light from the oil-lamp created an atmosphere of mystery. Policemen could be heard searching the park and raking the gravel.

As for Else, she scarcely dared to go over to her brother, holding herself rigid, when Maigret ordered her to do so.

'I think he's in a bad way,' whispered Lucas.

She must have heard. She looked at him, hesitating to go nearer Carl who gazed at her intently and tried to lift himself up on his bed.

Then she burst into tears, ran out of the room, went back into her own room, and threw herself, shaking with sobs, on to her divan.

Maigret motioned to the sergeant to watch her and gave his attention to the wounded man, taking off his jacket and waistcoat with the gestures of a man used to this sort of incident.

'Don't worry . . . We've sent for a doctor . . . Else is in her room . . .'

Andersen remained silent, as if overwhelmed by a mysterious anxiety. He looked round him, giving the impression that he was trying to solve an enigma, to discover some solemn secret.

'I'll question you later on . . . But . . .'

Bending down to examine the Dane's bare torso, the Chief-Inspector frowned.

'You've been hit by two bullets . . . This wound in the back is anything but recent . . .'

And it was a horrible sight. Four square inches of skin had been shot away. The flesh was literally chopped up, burnt, blistered, and caked with crusts of congealed blood. This wound had stopped bleeding, which proved that it had been inflicted several hours before.

On the other hand another bullet had recently smashed the left shoulder-blade, and in the course of washing the wound Maigret extracted the bullet. It fell on to the floor and he picked it up.

It was not a revolver bullet but a rifle bullet, like the one which had killed Madame Goldberg.

'Where is Else?' murmured the wounded man, who was managing not to grimace with pain.

'In her room . . . Don't move . . . Did you see who shot you just now?'

'No.'

'And the other time? . . . Where was it?'

The forehead creased. Andersen opened his mouth to say something but wearily gave up the attempt, while his left arm, with a mere hint of movement, tried to explain that he was no longer capable of talking.

80

'What are your conclusions, Doctor?'

It was irritating, living in this semi-darkness. There were only two oil-lamps in the house, one of which had been placed in the wounded man's room and the other in Else's.

Downstairs a candle had been lit which did not light up a quarter of the drawing-room.

'Unless there are some unforeseen complications, he'll pull round . . . The more serious wound is the first . . . It must have been inflicted in the early afternoon or late morning . . . A bullet fired into the back from a Browning at point-blank range. And I mean point-blank range! . . . Indeed I shouldn't be surprised if the muzzle of the revolver had been touching the flesh. The victim made a sudden movement . . . The bullet was deflected and the ribs are about all that was hit . . . There are bruises on the shoulder and the arms, and scratches on the hands and knees which must have occurred at the same time . . .'

'And the other bullet?'

'The shoulder-blade has been smashed. He'll have to have an operation tomorrow . . . I can give you the address of a clinic in Paris . . . There's one in the district, but if the patient has money I would advise Paris . . .'

'Could he move about after the first shooting?'

'Probably . . . Seeing that no vital organ had been hit, it was really just a matter of will-power and energy . . . But I'm afraid he'll have a stiff shoulder for the rest of his life . . .'

In the park the policemen had found nothing, but they had stationed themselves in such a way as to make it possible to organize a thorough search at daybreak.

A few moments later Maigret went back to Andersen, who was obviously relieved to see him come in.

'Else?'

'In her room, I've already told you twice.'

'Why?'

Again that morbid anxiety, which was visible in every one of the Dane's glances and in the twitching of his features.

'You don't know of any enemies you might have?'

'No.'

'Don't get excited . . . Just tell me how you got shot the first time . . . Take it easy . . . Don't tire yourself . . .'

'I was on my way to Dumas's . . .'

'You didn't show up there . . .'

'I meant to! . . . At the Porte d'Orléans a man signalled me to stop my motor . . .'

He asked for something to drink, emptied a large glass of water, and looking at the ceiling, went on:

'He told me he belonged to the police. He even showed me a card, which I didn't look at. He ordered me to cross Paris and take the road to Compiègne, saying that I was going to be confronted with a witness. He got into the motor beside me.'

'What did he look like?'

'Tall, with a soft grey hat. Just before you get to Compiègne, the main road goes through a forest . . . As I was taking a bend, I felt something hit me in the back . . . A hand grabbed the steering-wheel which I was holding, and I was pushed out of the motor . . . I fainted . . . I came to in the ditch . . . The motor had gone . . .'

'What time was it?'

'Perhaps eleven in the morning . . . I don't know . . . The clock in the motor doesn't work . . . I went into the wood, to pull myself together and to have time to think . . . I kept feeling faint . . . I heard trains going by . . . I ended up by finding a little station. At five o'clock I was in Paris, where I took a room in a hotel. I had a wash and tidied up my clothes . . . Finally I came here . . .'

'Concealing your movements . . .'

'Yes.'

'Why?'

'I don't know.'

'Did you meet anybody?'

'No. I came in through the park, without going along the main road . . . Just as I was getting near the steps, somebody fired a shot . . . I'd like to see Else . . .'

'Do you know that somebody has tried to poison her?'

Maigret was a long way from expecting the effect which these words obtained. The Dane sat up with a single movement, stared intently at him, and stammered:

'Really?'

And he looked overjoyed, as if he had been freed from a nightmare.

'I want to see her!'

Maigret went into the corridor and found Else in her room, stretched out on the divan, her eyes vacant, opposite Lucas who was watching her closely.

'Come along, will you?'

'What has he said?'

She was still hesitant, afraid. In the wounded man's room she took a couple of faltering steps, then rushed across to Carl and hugged him, talking to him in her own language.

Lucas eyed Maigret gloomily.

'Can *you* make anything of it?'

The Chief-Inspector shrugged his shoulders, and instead of answering started giving orders.

'Make sure the garage-proprietor hasn't left Paris . . . Ring up the Prefecture and tell them to send a surgeon along first thing tomorrow . . . Or tonight if possible . . .'

'Where are you going?'

'I haven't the faintest idea. Keep up the watch on the park, but it won't give us any results.'

He returned to the ground floor, went down the flight of

steps, and reached the main road, all alone. The garage was closed, but the milky disks of the petrol-pumps were glowing.

There was a light on the first floor of the Michonnets' villa. Behind the blind the silhouette of the insurance agent was still in the same place.

It was a cool night. A thin mist was rising from the fields and forming wraiths which floated in the air about three feet from the ground. Somewhere in the direction of Arpajon there was the noise of a motor and some old iron coming nearer. Five minutes later a lorry drew up in front of the garage and sounded its horn.

A little door opened in the iron shutter, showing the electric light bulb burning inside.

'Twenty litres!'

The sleepy mechanic worked the pump while the driver stayed up in his cab. The Chief-Inspector came up, his hands in his pockets, his pipe between his teeth.

'Isn't Monsieur Oscar back yet?'

'Oh, it's you! ... No. When he goes to Paris, he doesn't come back till the following morning ...'

He hesitated, then said:

'Look, Arthur, you'd better take your spare wheel. It's ready for you.'

And the mechanic went into the garage to get a wheel fitted with a tyre, rolled it up to the lorry, and laboriously fastened it to the back.

The lorry moved off. Its red lamp faded into the distance. The mechanic stretched himself and sighed:

'Are you still looking for the murderer? ... At this time of night? ... Well, all I can say is that if I was allowed to get a bit of shut-eye I wouldn't care about anybody!'

A clock struck two.

A train trailed a plume of smoke along the horizon.

'Are you coming in or staying out?'

And the man stretched himself, impatient to get back to bed.

Maigret went in and looked at the whitewashed walls on which there were nails holding red inner tubes and tyres of various brands, most of them in poor condition.

'Look here . . . What's he going to do with the wheel you've given him?'

'Eh? . . . Put it on his lorry, of course!'

'You think so? . . . Then his lorry's going to give him a bumpy ride . . . Because that wheel isn't the same diameter as the others.'

A worried look appeared in the man's eyes.

'Perhaps I made a mistake . . . Wait a minute . . . Did I give him the wheel from old Mathieu's van? . . .'

There was an explosion. It was Maigret who had just fired at one of the inner tubes hanging on the wall. And the tube went flat, letting some little white paper packets drop through the hole.

'Don't you move, my lad!'

For the mechanic, bent double, was on the point of running at him head first.

'Mind out, or I'll fire.'

'What do you want?'

'Hands up! . . . Quicker than that!'

And he moved swiftly over to Jojo, felt his pockets, and took charge of a revolver loaded with six bullets.

'Go and lie down on your camp-bed . . .'

Maigret kicked the door shut. Looking at the mechanic's freckled face, he saw that the man was not resigning himself to defeat.

'Lie down.'

He could not see any rope around him, but he noticed a coil of electric wire.

'Your hands!'

As Maigret had to let go of his revolver, the mechanic made a sudden movement, but only to receive the Chief-Inspector's fist full in the face. His nose started bleeding. His lip puffed up. The man gave a snarl of fury. His hands were tied and soon his feet were bound too.

'How old are you?'

'Twenty-one.'

'And where have you come from?'

A silence. Maigret simply had to show his fist.

'The reform school at Montpellier.'

'Good. You know what's inside these little packets?'

'Drugs.'

The voice was bad-tempered. The mechanic was flexing his muscles in the hope of snapping the electric wire.

'What was there in the spare wheel?'

'I don't know.'

'Then why did you give it to that lorry rather than another?'

'I'm not answering any more questions!'

'So much the worse for you!'

Five inner tubes were punctured one after another, but not all of them contained cocaine. In one, which had a patch covering a long tear, Maigret found some silver cutlery engraved with a marquess's coronet. In another there was some lace and antique jewellery.

There were ten motor-cars in the garage. Only one worked when Maigret tried to start them, one after another. Then, armed with a monkey-wrench, and occasionally using a hammer as well, he proceeded to break up the engines and cut open the petrol tanks.

The mechanic watched him with a sneer on his face.

'You can't say we aren't well stocked, can you?' he said.

The petrol tank of a four-horse-power motor was stuffed

with bearer bonds. At the very lowest estimate there were three hundred thousand francs' worth.

'Does that come from the Savings Bank robbery?'

'Maybe.'

'And these old coins?'

'Don't know . . .'

There was more variety than in the back room of a junkshop. There was something of everything: pearls, banknotes, American currency, and official stamps which must have been used to forge false passports.

Maigret could not break everything. But, ripping open the sagging cushions of a saloon car, he found some silver florins, which was enough to convince him that everything in the garage was a sham.

A lorry went by along the road without stopping. A quarter of an hour later, another drove past the garage and the Chief-Inspector frowned.

He was beginning to understand how the organization worked. The garage stood on the main road, thirty miles from Paris, within easy reach of big provincial towns such as Chartres, Orléans, Le Mans, and Châteaudun.

There were no neighbours, except for the occupants of the house of the Three Widows and the Michonnets' villa.

What could they see?

A thousand vehicles went past every day. A hundred of them at least stopped in front of the petrol-pumps. A few drove in for running repairs. Tyres and wheels were sold or changed. Cans of oil and drums of diesel oil changed hands.

One detail was particularly interesting: every evening, heavy lorries went by on their way to Paris, loaded with vegetables for the Central Market. Late in the night, or in the morning, they came back empty.

Empty? . . . Wasn't it those lorries which, in their baskets and crates, carried the stolen goods?

It could well be a regular daily service. A single tyre, the one containing cocaine, was enough to indicate the scale of the traffic, for there was over two hundred thousand francs' worth of drugs in it.

And on top of all that, the garage was probably used for disguising stolen motor-cars.

No witnesses. Monsieur Oscar standing in the doorway, with his hands in his pockets. Mechanics busy with monkey-wrenches or blow-lamps. The five red-and-white petrol-pumps providing a respectable front.

Didn't the butcher, the baker, the passing tourist stop like everybody else?

A clock struck in the distance. Maigret looked at his watch. It was half past three.

'Who's your boss?' he asked without looking at his prisoner.

The other only grinned in reply.

'You know very well you'll end up by talking . . . Is it Monsieur Oscar? . . . What's his real name?'

'Oscar.'

The mechanic looked as if he were on the point of bursting out laughing.

'Did Monsieur Goldberg come here?'

'Who's he?'

'You know as well as I do! The Belgian who was murdered . . .?'

'You don't say!'

'Who was given the job of bumping off the Dane on the Compiègne road?'

'Has somebody been bumped off?'

There was no room for doubt. Maigret's first impression was confirmed. He was dealing with a well-organized gang of professional criminals.

He was given fresh proof of this. The noise of a motor on

the road came nearer, and a vehicle stopped in front of the iron shutter with a squeal of brakes, while the horn sounded a summons.

Maigret ran forward. But before he had opened the door the motor-car had moved off at such speed that he could not even make out its shape.

His fists clenched, he came back towards the mechanic.

'How did you warn him?'

'Me?'

And the man laughed as he held out his wrists tied together with electric wire.

'Talk!'

'I suppose it smells funny here and that chap's got a good nose.'

Maigret was worried. Suddenly he overturned the camp-bed, throwing Jojo on to the ground, for he thought that there might be an electric switch working a warning signal outside.

But he found nothing under the bed. He left the man on the ground, went out, and saw the five petrol-pumps lit up as usual.

He was beginning to lose his temper.

'Isn't there a phone in the garage?'

'Look for yourself!'

'You know you'll end up by talking . . .'

'Blab away!'

There was no hope of getting anything out of the fellow, who was a typical hardened criminal. For a quarter of an hour Maigret paced up and down fifty yards of roadway, vainly looking for something which might be serving as a signal.

In the Michonnets' villa the light on the first floor had gone out. Only the house of the Three Widows was still lit up and over there you could sense the presence of the policemen surrounding the park.

A limousine roared past.

'What sort of motor does your boss drive?'

Dawn appeared in the east in the form of a whitish mist which barely showed over the horizon.

Maigret stared at the mechanic's hands. They were not touching anything which could send a signal.

A draught of fresh air came in through the little door open in the corrugated iron shutter of the garage.

And yet, just as Maigret, hearing the sound of a motor, walked towards the road and saw a four-seater touring-car driving up which was not doing more than twenty miles an hour and looked as if it were going to stop, a positive fusillade broke out.

Several men were firing and the bullets rattled against the corrugated shutter.

There was nothing to be seen but the glare of the head-lamps and motionless shadows, or rather heads, showing above the bodywork of the motor. Then came the roar of the accelerator . . .

Broken windows . . .

That was on the first floor of the house of the Three Widows. The men had gone on firing from the motor . . .

Maigret, who had thrown himself flat on the ground, stood up, his mouth dry, his pipe out.

He was sure that he had recognized Monsieur Oscar at the wheel of the motor which had plunged back into the darkness.

CHAPTER 8

The Vanishing Trick

THE Chief-Inspector had barely had time to reach the middle of the road before a taxi appeared and braked hard in front of the petrol-pumps. A man jumped out and collided with Maigret.

'Grandjean!' growled the Chief-Inspector.

'Petrol, quick!'

The taxi-driver was pale with nervous strain, for he had just been driving at sixty miles an hour a motor-car intended to do fifty at the very most.

Grandjean belonged to the Highways Squad. There were two other inspectors with him in the taxi. Each fist was gripping a revolver.

The petrol tank was filled in a feverish hurry.

'Are they far away?'

'Three or four miles ahead of you.'

The driver was waiting for the order to drive on.

'You stay here,' Maigret told Grandjean. 'The other two can go on without you . . .'

And he urged them:

'Don't take any risks! . . . We've got them anyway . . . Just follow them . . .'

The taxi drove off. A loose mudguard clattered along the road.

'Tell me all about it, Grandjean!'

And Maigret listened, at the same time watching the three houses, registering the noises of the night, and keeping an eye on the captive mechanic.

'It was Lucas who phoned me to tell me to watch the proprietor of this garage, Monsieur Oscar ... I started trailing him at the Porte d'Orléans ... They had a big dinner at the Escargot, where they didn't speak to anybody, and then they went to the Ambigu ... So far nothing interesting ... At midnight they left the theatre and I saw them making for the Chope Saint-Martin ... You know the place ... There are always a few lascars upstairs, in the little dining-room ... Monsieur Oscar went in there as if the place belonged to him ... The waiters fussed over him, the manager shook hands with him, asked him how his business was going ... As for his wife, she looked as if she was in her element too.

'They sat down at a table where there were already three blokes and a tart ... I recognized one of the blokes as an iron-merchant somewhere in the République district ... Another runs a junk-shop in the rue du Temple ... I don't know about the third, but the tart who was with him is bound to be in the Vice Squad records ...

'They started drinking champagne and laughing and joking. Then they ordered crayfish, onion soup, heaven knows what else besides. A real blow-out, the kind that sort like, shouting, slapping their thighs, and singing a ditty every now and then ...

'There was a jealousy scene because Monsieur Oscar was squeezing up against the tart and his wife didn't like her ... It was all smoothed out in the end with another bottle of champagne ...

'From time to time the manager came to have a drink with his customers and he even treated them to a round ... Then, about three o'clock, I think, the waiter came to say that Monsieur Oscar was wanted on the phone ...

'When he came back from the call-box he'd stopped laughing. He gave me a dirty look, because I was the only customer who wasn't in his gang ... He talked to the others in a whisper ... They were in a nice mess! ... They all pulled faces as long as your arm . . . Monsieur Oscar's wife had rings under her eyes down to the middle of her cheeks and she emptied her glass to buck herself up . . .

'There was only one bloke who followed the pair of them, the one I don't know, an Italian or Spaniard by the look of him . . .

'While they were saying their fond farewells I nipped out on to the boulevard. I picked a taxi that didn't look too much of a wreck and I called up two inspectors who were on duty at the Porte Saint-Denis . . .

'You've seen their motor . . . Well, they started driving at sixty miles an hour along the Boulevard Saint-Michel. They were whistled at at least a dozen times without stopping . . . We had the devil of a job following them . . . The taxi-driver – he's a Russian – said that I was making him burn up his engine . . .'

'Was it them who fired?'

'Yes.'

Lucas had had time, after hearing the fusillade, to leave the house of the Three Widows and join the Chief-Inspector.

'What's happened?'

'How's Andersen?'

'He's weaker. All the same, I think he'll hold out till the morning . . . The surgeon is due to arrive soon. But what's this?'

Lucas was looking at the garage's bullet-scarred shutter and the camp-bed on which the mechanic was still tied up with his electric wire.

'An organized gang, eh, Chief?'

'And how!'

Maigret was more worried than usual. That showed particularly in a slight hunching of the shoulders. His lips were creased in a peculiar fold around the stem of his pipe.

'You, Lucas, go and spread the net . . . Phone to Arpajon,

Étampes, Chartres, Orléans, Le Mans, Rambouillet ... You'd better have a look at the map ... Get every police station on its toes ... Road-blocks up outside the towns ... We've got that little lot where we want them ... What's Else Andersen doing?'

'I don't know ... I left her in her room ... She's very depressed ...'

'You don't say!' retorted Maigret with unexpected sarcasm.

They were still standing in the road.

'Where shall I phone from?'

'There's a phone in the corridor in the garage-proprietor's house ... Start with Orléans, because they'll have gone through Étampes already ...'

A light appeared in an isolated farm in the midst of the fields. The peasants were getting up. A lantern moved round a wall and disappeared, and then it was the turn of the cow-shed windows to light up.

'Five o'clock ... They're starting to milk the cows ...'

Lucas had moved off, and was forcing open the door of Monsieur Oscar's house with the aid of a crowbar he had picked up in the garage.

As for Grandjean, he followed Maigret without really understanding what it was all about.

'The latest developments are as clear as daylight,' muttered the Chief-Inspector. 'There's only the beginning to sort out ...'

'Now I come to think of it, there's a fellow up there who sent for me just to show me that he was incapable of walking. Four hours now he has been in the same place, motionless, absolutely motionless ...

'Because the windows are lit up, aren't they! And there was I, just now, looking for the signal! ... You can't understand ... The lorries going past without stopping ...

'You see, the window wasn't lit up then!'

Maigret burst out laughing as if he had found out something excruciatingly funny.

And suddenly his companion saw him take a revolver out of his pocket and aim it at the Michonnets' window in which could be seen the shadow of a head resting against the back of an armchair.

The sound of the shot was as sharp as the crack of a whip. It was followed by the tinkling of broken glass falling into the garden.

But nothing moved in the bedroom. The shadow retained exactly the same shape behind the canvas blind.

'What did you do that for?'

'Break the door down! . . . No, ring the bell! . . . I'd be surprised if nobody came to the door.'

Nobody came. They could not hear anything inside.

'Break it down!'

Grandjean was a great hulk of a man. He took a running jump and hurled himself three times at the door, which finally gave way, its hinges torn off.

'Take it easy . . . Careful . . .'

Each had a gun in his hand. The light-switch in the dining-room was the first to be turned. The table, which was covered with a red check tablecloth, was still littered with the dirty plates from dinner and a decanter containing a little white wine. Maigret drank it out of the decanter.

There was nothing in the drawing-room. Dust sheets over the armchairs. The fusty atmosphere of a room that is never lived in.

A cat was the only creature to run out of the white-tiled kitchen.

The inspector was looking anxiously at Maigret. Eventually they went upstairs to the first floor, where there were three doors surrounding the landing.

The Chief-Inspector opened the door of the bedroom at the front of the house.

A draught coming from the broken window was stirring the blind. In the armchair they saw a comical thing, a broomstick propped up at an angle, with one end wrapped in a bundle of rags which, showing above the back of the armchair, looked like a head when seen in silhouette from outside.

Maigret did not even smile, but opened a communicating door and switched on the light in a second bedroom which was empty.

The top floor. An attic with apples laid on the floor about one inch from one another and strings of French beans hanging from the beam. A bedroom which was obviously a maid's room but which was not used, for there was nothing in it but an old bedside table.

They went downstairs again. Maigret crossed the kitchen and went out into the yard. It faced east and in that direction the dirty halo of dawn was growing larger.

A small shed . . . A door which moved slightly . . .

'Who's there?' he shouted brandishing his revolver.

There was a squeal of terror. The door, which was no longer being held from inside, swung open to reveal a woman who fell on her knees, crying:

'I haven't done anything! . . . I'm sorry! . . . I . . . I . . .'

It was Madame Michonnet, her hair tousled, her clothes spattered with plaster from the shed.

'Where's your husband?'

'I don't know . . . I swear I don't know . . . I'm miserable enough as it is . . .'

She was crying. The whole of her plump body seemed to be softening, collapsing. Her face looked ten years older than usual, swollen with tears, decomposed by fear.

'It isn't me! . . . I haven't done anything! . . . It's that man across the road . . .'

'Which man?'

'The foreigner ... I don't know anything about it ... But it's him, you can be sure of that! ... My husband isn't a murderer or a thief ... He's got a life of honesty behind him ... It's that man with the evil eye ... Ever since he came to the crossroads, everything's gone wrong ... I ...'

There was a hen-house full of white hens pecking at the ground which was covered with big yellow grains of corn. The cat had perched on a window sill and its eyes were shining in the semi-darkness.

'Get up.'

'What are you going to do with me? Who fired those shots?'

It was pitiful. She was nearly fifty and she was crying like a child. She was utterly distraught, to such an extent that when she had got to her feet and Maigret unconsciously patted her on the back, she practically threw herself into his arms, and laid her head on his chest, clutching the lapels of his jacket and groaning:

'I'm just a poor woman, I am! ... I've worked all my life! ... When I got married, I was the cashier in the biggest hotel in Montpellier ...'

Maigret gently pushed her away, but he could not put a stop to her plaintive confidences.

'I'd have done better to stay as I was ... Because people looked up to me ... When I left, I remember that the boss, who thought a lot of me, told me I'd be sorry ... And it's true ... I've had to slave away harder than ever ...'

She broke down again. The sight of her cat revived her distress.

'Poor Pussy! ... You've got nothing to do with all this either! ... And my hens, my kitchen, my home! ... You know, Chief-Inspector, I do believe I could kill that man if he was here in front of me! ... I felt it the first day I saw him ... Just the sight of those black eyes of his ...'

'Where's your husband?'

'How should I know?'

'He went off early last night, didn't he? Straight after I'd been to see him . . . He wasn't any iller than I am . . .'

She did not know what to say in reply. Her eyes darted around as if she was looking for support.

'He suffers from gout, that's certain . . .'

'Has Mademoiselle Else ever been here?'

'Never!' she exclaimed indignantly. 'I won't have any women like that in my house . . .'

'And Monsieur Oscar?'

'Have you arrested him?'

'Nearly.'

'He deserves it too . . . My husband shouldn't have had anything to do with people who aren't our sort, people without any education . . . Oh, if only men would listen to their wives . . . What do you think is going to happen . . . I keep hearing shots all the time . . . If anything happened to Michonnet I think I'd die of shame . . . Not to mention the fact that I'm too old to start working again . . .'

'Go back into the house.'

'What have I got to do?'

'Have a hot drink . . . Wait . . . Sleep if you can . . .'

'Sleep?'

This word brought on a fresh deluge, a flood of tears, but one which she had to finish on her own, for the two men had gone out.

Maigret, however, came back and unhooked the receiver of the telephone.

'Hullo. Arpajon? This is the police. Will you tell me what numbers have been asked for on this line during the night?'

He had to wait a few minutes. Finally the answer was given to him.

'Archives 27-45 ... It's a big café near the Porte Saint-Martin ...'

'I know ... Have you had any other calls from the Three Widows Crossroads?'

'Just now from the garage. They wanted some police stations ...'

'Thank you!'

When Maigret rejoined Inspector Grandjean on the road, a drizzle as fine as mist was falling. All the same, the sky was turning milky-white.

'Can you make anything of it, Chief-Inspector?'

'More or less.'

'That woman's putting it on isn't she?'

'She's being absolutely honest ...'

'But her husband ...'

'Oh, he's another matter. A good sort who's gone to the bad. Or, if you like, a criminal who was born to be a good sort ... There's nothing more complicated than people like that ... They worry for hours trying to find a way out of the mess ... They think up the most fantastic plans ... And they can put on a wonderful act ... For instance, I'd like to know what, at a given moment in his life, made him set up as a criminal, so to speak ... I'd also like to know what he managed to think up for last night ...'

Maigret filled his pipe and went up to the gate of the house of the Three Widows. There was a policeman on guard there.

'No news?'

'I don't think they've found anything ... The park is surrounded ... We haven't seen anybody, though.'

The two men walked round the building which was turning a yellowish colour in the half-light, while the details of its architecture were beginning to stand out.

The big drawing-room was in exactly the same state as on

Maigret's first visit: the easel still held a sketch for a design with big crimson flowers. A record on the gramophone was sending out two tapering gleams of light. The dawn was filtering into the room like a swirling mist.

The same stairs creaked. In his bedroom, Carl Andersen, who had been groaning when the Chief-Inspector arrived, fell silent as soon as he saw him, mastering his pain but not his impatience.

'Where's Else?' he stammered.

'In her room.'

'Ah . . .'

That seemed to reassure him. He gave a sigh and felt his shoulder, frowning slightly.

'I don't think this is going to kill me . . .'

It was his glass eye which was the most painful thing to look at, because it did not participate in the life of his face. It remained wide open, clear and still, while all his muscles were moving.

'I'd rather she didn't see me like this . . . Do you think my shoulder will mend? . . . Have they sent for a good surgeon?'

He too had become a child in his distress, like Madame Michonnet. There was a look of entreaty in his eyes. He wanted to be reassured. But what seemed to be preoccupying him most of all was his looks, the traces the recent incidents might leave on his physical appearance.

On the other hand he was showing extraordinary will-power, a remarkable capacity for mastering pain. Maigret, who had seen his two wounds, could appreciate this.

'Tell Else . . .'

'You don't want to see her?'

'No. Better not. But tell her that I'm going to get better, that . . . I'm in full possession of my faculties, that she must have faith. Repeat that word to her: faith! . . . Tell her to read a few verses of the Bible . . . The story of Job, for instance

100

. . . That makes you smile, because the French don't know the Bible . . . Faith! . . . "*I shall always know my own*." That is God speaking, God who knows His own . . . Tell her that . . . And this too: "*There will be more joy in heaven over* . . ." She will understand . . . And finally: "*The righteous man is tested nine times a day*" . . .'

It was incredible. Wounded, racked with pain, lying between a couple of policemen, he was serenely quoting from the Scriptures.

'Faith . . . You'll tell her, won't you? . . . Because there is no precedent for innocence . . .'

He frowned. He had noticed a smile hovering on Inspector Grandjean's lips. And then he muttered to himself, between his teeth:

'*Franzose!*'

'*Frenchman!*' In other words, unbeliever, sceptic, trifler, scoffer!

Discouraged, he turned his face to the wall, staring at it with his one living eye.

*

'Tell her . . .'

But when Maigret and his companion pushed open the door of Else's bedroom, they found nobody there.

A hot-house atmosphere. An opaque cloud of cigarette smoke. And a feminine aroma you could cut with a knife, calculated to turn a schoolboy's head or even a man's.

But not a living soul . . . The window was shut. Else had not got out that way.

The picture hiding the hole in the wall, the bottle of tablets, the key, and the revolver was in its place.

Maigret pushed it to one side. The revolver was missing.

'Oh, stop looking at me like that, dammit!'

And Maigret, as he said this, threw an exasperated glance

at the inspector who was standing behind him gazing at him in blissful admiration.

At that moment the Chief-Inspector bit on the stem of his pipe so hard that he broke it and the bowl dropped on to the floor.

'She's done a bunk?'

'Shut up!'

He was furious, unfair. Grandjean was hurt and stood as still as possible.

Dawn had not yet broken. There was still the same grey mist floating about at ground-level but not shedding any light. The baker's motor went by along the road, an old Ford whose front wheels wobbled on the asphalt.

All of a sudden Maigret dashed into the corridor and ran downstairs. And at the very moment that he reached the drawing-room, where two windows were standing wide open on to the park, there was a terrible cry, a cry of death, the plaintive howl of an animal in pain.

It was a woman who was crying out, her voice stifled by some unidentifiable object.

It was far away or very close. It could have come from the cornice, it could have come from under the ground.

And there was such a feeling of terror that the man on guard at the gate ran up looking absolutely distraught.

'Chief-Inspector! . . . Did you hear that cry?'

'Shut up, damn you!' yelled Maigret, beside himself with exasperation.

The words were scarcely out of his mouth before a shot was heard, but so muffled that nobody could have said whether it was to the left or the right, in the park, in the house, in the wood, or on the road.

Then came the sound of footsteps on the stairs, and they saw Carl Andersen coming down, holding himself erect with one hand on his chest, and shouting like a madman:

'It's her!'

He was panting for breath. His glass eye remained motion-less. Nobody could tell at whom he was staring with the other wide-open eye.

CHAPTER 9

The Man in a Row

THERE was a pause of a few seconds, roughly long enough to allow the last echoes of the shot to die away in the air. They waited for another. Carl Andersen walked forward until he came to a gravel path.

It was one of the policemen mounting guard in the park who suddenly rushed towards the kitchen garden, in the middle of which there stood the lip of a well surmounted by a pulley. He had scarcely bent over before he flung himself backwards and blew his whistle.

'Take him away, by force if necessary!' Maigret shouted to Lucas, pointing to the tottering Dane.

It all happened at once, in the dim light of dawn. Lucas motioned to one of his men. The two of them went up to the wounded man, parleyed with him for a moment, and then, since Carl would not hear reason, pushed him over and carried him off, struggling and gasping out hoarse protests.

Maigret ran up to the well, only to be stopped by the policeman, who shouted:

'Mind out!'

A bullet whistled past, while the underground explosion was continued by prolonged reverberations.

'Who is it?'

'The girl . . . And a man . . . They're fighting like mad.'

The Chief-Inspector approached cautiously. But he could see scarcely anything.

'Your torch . . .'

He had time only to form a sketchy impression of what was happening, for a bullet nearly shattered the torch.

The man was Michonnet. The well was not very deep. On the other hand it was wide and dried up.

And there were two of them, fighting in it. As far as Maigret could see, the insurance agent was holding Else by the throat as if he were trying to strangle her. She had a revolver in her hand. But he was gripping that hand of hers too, and aiming the shots as he wished.

'What are we going to do?' asked the inspector.

He was horrified. A groan came up to them every now and then. It was Else who was choking and struggling desperately.

'Michonnet, give yourself up!' Maigret called out as a matter of form.

The other man did not even answer, but fired into the air, and the Chief-Inspector did not hesitate any longer. The well was nine foot deep. Maigret suddenly jumped over the edge and literally fell on the insurance agent's back, trapping one of Else's legs in the process.

There was utter confusion. Another bullet went off, ricocheted off the side of the well, and disappeared into the sky while the Chief-Inspector, out of prudence, hammered away with both fists on Michonnet's skull.

At the fourth blow the insurance agent darted the glance of a wounded animal at him, swayed on his feet, and fell backwards, with one black eye and his jaw dislocated.

Else, who was holding her throat with both hands, was making an effort to breathe.

It was at once tragic and grotesque, this battle at the bottom of a well, in the half-light and a smell of saltpetre and slime.

The epilogue was even more grotesque: Michonnet, who was hauled up with the aid of the pulley, soft, limp, and groaning; Else whom Maigret hoisted up himself, and who was filthy, with her black velvet dress covered with big patches of greenish moss.

Neither she nor her adversary had completely lost consciousness. But they were exhausted and dejected, like those clowns whom you see parodying a boxing-match and who, lying on top of one another, go on aimlessly punching the air.

Maigret had picked up the revolver. It was Else's, the one missing from the hiding-place in the bedroom. There was one bullet left in it.

Lucas arrived from the house looking worried, and sighed at the sight which met his eyes.

'I had to tie the other fellow to his bed . . .'

The policeman was dabbing the girl's forehead with a handkerchief soaked in water. The sergeant asked:

'Where have these two come from?'

He had scarcely finished speaking before Michonnet, who had not even the strength left to stand up, nonetheless threw himself at Else, his face convulsed with rage. He did not have time to reach her. Giving him a kick which sent him rolling six feet away, Maigret shouted at him:

'Have you finished your little game yet?'

Then he started laughing uncontrollably, the expression on the insurance agent's face was so comical. It made him think of those angry children whom you carry off under your arm, spanking them as you go, and who go on struggling, howling and crying, trying to bite you and hit you, without admitting their helplessness.

For Michonnet was crying! He was crying and shaking his fist!

Else had at last got to her feet and was passing her hand over her forehead.

'I really thought I was done for then!' she sighed with a wan smile. 'He was squeezing so hard . . .'

One of her cheeks was black with earth, and there was mud in her tousled hair. Maigret was scarcely any cleaner.

'What were you doing in the well?' he asked.

She darted a piercing glance at him. Her smile vanished. He could tell that, at a single stroke, she had regained all her self-possession.

'Answer me!'

'I . . . I was carried there forcibly . . .'

'By Michonnet?'

'That's a lie!' shouted the insurance agent.

'It's the truth . . . He tried to strangle me . . . I think he's insane.'

'She's lying . . . She's the one that's insane . . . Or rather she . . .'

'She what?'

'I don't know. She . . . She's a viper, whose head ought to be smashed against a stone . . .'

Dawn had broken imperceptibly. Birds were chirping in all the trees.

'Why had you got a revolver with you?'

'Because I was afraid of a trap . . .'

'What trap? . . . Wait a minute! . . . Let's take things one at a time . . . You've just said that you were attacked and carried into the well . . .'

'She's lying!' the insurance agent repeated in a voice choking with anger.

'Show me,' Maigret went on, 'the place where this attack took place.'

She looked around her and pointed to the flight of steps.

'It was there? And you didn't scream for help?'

'I couldn't.'

'And this skinny little fellow managed to carry you as far as the well, in other words to cover two hundred yards with a load weighing eight stone?'

'That's the truth . . .'

'She's lying!'

'Tell him to shut up,' she said wearily. 'Can't you see that he's mad?... And it didn't start today...'

They had to restrain Michonnet, who was going to rush at her again.

They formed a small group in the garden: Maigret, Lucas, and a couple of inspectors, looking at the insurance agent with the swollen face and at Else who, while she was talking, was trying to tidy herself up.

It would have been hard to say why the scene did not manage to attain the level of tragedy or even of drama. It savoured rather of farce.

Perhaps that dim dawn light had something to do with it? And also every body's fatigue, even hunger?

It was worse when they saw a woman walking hesitantly along the road, peering through the bars of the gate, opening it, and exclaiming as she looked at Michonnet:

'Émile!'

It was Madame Michonnet, more exhausted than distressed, Madame Michonnet who took a handkerchief out of her pocket and burst into tears.

'With that woman again!'

She looked like a plump, kindly mother shaken by events and taking refuge in the comforting bitterness of tears.

Maigret noticed with amusement the clear-cut appearance which Else's face was taking on as she looked at each person in turn. A pretty face, very thin, and suddenly tense and pointed.

'What were you going to do in the well?' he asked in a good-natured way, as if he were saying:

'You've finished stalling, haven't you? Between us two, there isn't any point in going on with the act.'

She understood. Her lips stretched in an ironic smile.

'I reckon we're caught like rats in a trap,' she conceded. 'Only I'm hungry and thirsty and cold, and in spite of everything I'd like to tidy up... After that, we'll see...'

She was not play-acting. On the contrary she was being admirably clear.

She was all alone in the middle of the group but she was perfectly at ease. She looked with an amused expression at the weeping Madame Michonnet and the pitiful Michonnet. Then she turned towards Maigret and her eyes said:

'The poor devils! We two belong to the same class, don't we? ... We'll have a chat later on ... You've won! ... But you must admit that I gave you a good run for your money!'

No fear and no embarrassment either. Not the slightest trace of histrionics.

It was the real Else who had at last come to the surface and who was savouring this revelation herself.

'Come with me,' said Maigret. 'You take care of Michonnet, Lucas ... As for his wife, she can go back home or stay here ...'

*

'Come in! I don't mind ...'

It was the same bedroom upstairs, with the black divan, the powerful scent, the hiding-place behind the water-colour. It was the same woman.

'Carl is well guarded, I hope?' she said, jerking her head towards the wounded man's room. 'Because he'd be even wilder than Michonnet ... You can smoke your pipe ...'

She poured some water into the bowl, calmly took off her dress as if it were the most natural thing in the world, and stood there in her slip, neither modest nor provocative.

Maigret thought of his first visit to the house of the Three Widows, of the Else who had been as enigmatic and distant as a cinema vamp, of that strange, enervating atmosphere with which she managed to surround herself.

How well she had played the wilful girl of good family

when she had talked about her parents' castle, her nannies and governesses, her father's strict discipline.

It was all over. A single gesture was more eloquent than any number of words: the way in which she had taken off her dress and was now looking at herself in the mirror before washing her face.

She was the typical tart, ordinary and vulgar, healthy and cunning.

'You must admit that you fell for it!'

'Not for long.'

She wiped her face with one corner of a Turkish towel.

'You're boasting . . . Why, only yesterday, when you were here and I let you catch sight of one of my breasts, your mouth went dry and your forehead damp, like the good old fatty you are . . . Now, of course, you don't feel a thing . . . But I'm just as good-looking as I was . . .'

She straightened her back and looked complacently at her scantily clothed body.

'Between ourselves, what gave you the tip-off? Did I make a mistake?'

'Several . . .'

'What were they?'

'The mistake, for one thing, of talking a bit too much about the castle and the park . . . People who really live in a castle usually say the house . . .'

She had pulled aside the curtain of a hanging wardrobe and was looking hesitantly at her dresses.

'You're going to take me to Paris, aren't you? . . . And there'll be photographers there . . . What do you think of this green dress?'

She held it in front of her to judge the effect.

'No! It's still black that suits me best . . . Will you give me a light?'

She laughed, for, in spite of everything, Maigret was

disturbed by the subtle eroticism which she managed to inject into the atmosphere, especially when she came up to him to light her cigarette.

'Well, time to get dressed, I suppose . . . It's a scream, isn't it . . .'

Even slang expressions took on a special quality in her mouth, on account of her accent.

'How long have you been Carl Andersen's mistress?'

'I'm not his mistress. I'm his wife . . .'

She passed a pencil over her eyebrows and heightened the colour in her cheeks.

'You got married in Denmark?'

'You see? You still don't know a thing . . . And don't rely on me to talk . . . That wouldn't be fair . . . Besides, you won't have me for long . . . How soon after being arrested do I go through Records?'

'Straight away.'

'That's hard luck on you! . . . Because they'll find out that my real name is Bertha Krull and that the Copenhagen Police have had a warrant out for my arrest for just over three years . . . The Danish government will demand my extradition . . . There! I'm ready . . . Now, if you'll let me go and have a bite . . . Don't you think it smells musty in here?'

She went over to the window and opened it. Then she came back to the door. Maigret went out first. Then, all of a sudden, she slammed the door shut and shot the bolt home, and footsteps could be heard running towards the window.

If Maigret had been a stone or two lighter, she would probably have got away. He did not lose a second. The bolt had scarcely been shot before he threw the whole of his weight against the panel.

It gave way at the first blow. The door fell over, its lock and hinges torn off.

Else was sitting astride the window-sill. She hesitated.

'Too late!' he said.

She turned round, her breasts heaving slightly, her forehead damp with sweat.

'A lot of good it was getting all dolled up!' she said sarcastically, pointing to a tear in her dress.

'Will you give me your word that you won't try to run for it again?'

'No.'

'In that case, I warn you that I'll shoot at the slightest suspicious movement . . .'

And after that he kept his revolver in his hand.

As they were passing Carl's door she asked:

'Do you think he'll pull through? . . . He's got two bullets in him, hasn't he?'

He looked at her and at that particular moment he would have been hard put to it to come to any conclusion about her. But he thought that he could distinguish in her face and her voice a mixture of pity and spite.

'It's his fault too,' she concluded, as if to set her conscience at rest. 'Let's hope there's something left to eat in the house . . .'

Maigret followed her into the kitchen, where she rummaged about in the cupboards and finally came across a tin of crayfish.

'Will you open it for me? . . . Go on . . . I promise I won't take the opportunity to bolt for it . . .'

There was a sort of friendliness between them which Maigret did not fail to appreciate. There was even something intimate about their relationship, with just a hint of eroticism.

She enjoyed being with this big, even-tempered man who had defeated her but whom she was conscious of impressing with her pluck. As for him, he was savouring perhaps a little too much this promiscuity which was so unusual.

'Here you are . . . Eat up quickly.'

'Are we going already?'

'I haven't the faintest idea.'

'Between ourselves, what have you really found out?'

'It doesn't matter . . .'

'Are you taking that fool Michonnet along too? . . . He gave me the biggest fright of all . . . Just now, in the well, I really thought that I was done for . . . His eyes were popping out of his head . . . He was squeezing my throat as hard as he could . . .'

'Were you his mistress?'

She shrugged her shoulders, as a tart for whom that sort of detail is really very unimportant.

'And Monsieur Oscar?' he went on.

'Well, what about him?'

'Another lover?'

'You try to find all that out for yourself . . . Me, I know exactly what's waiting for me . . . I've got five years to do in Denmark for being involved in an armed robbery and insurrection . . . That's where I stopped this bullet . . .'

She pointed to her right breast.

'As for the rest, this lot here will have to face the music.'

'Where did you meet Isaac Goldberg?'

'I'm not talking . . .'

'You'll have to talk some time . . .'

'I'd like to know how you're going to make me . . .'

She answered while eating some crayfish without any bread, for there was none left in the house. A policeman could be heard walking up and down the drawing-room while watching Michonnet, who was slumped in an armchair.

Two motor-cars stopped at the same time outside the gate. After it had been opened, the motors drove into the park and round the house, stopping at the foot of the steps.

In the first motor there was an inspector, two gendarmes, Monsieur Oscar, and his wife.

The other motor was the taxi from Paris and in it an inspector was guarding a third individual.

All three had handcuffs on their wrists, but they looked calm and serene, except for the garage-proprietor's wife, who was red-eyed.

Maigret took Else into the drawing-room, where Michonnet made yet another attempt to rush at her.

The prisoners were brought in. Monsieur Oscar had almost the casual manner of an ordinary visitor, but he pulled a face when he caught sight of Else and the insurance agent. The other man, who looked like an Italian, decided to put on a swagger.

'A real family gathering! . . . Is it for a wedding or for the reading of a will.'

The inspector explained to Maigret.

'We're lucky to have nabbed them without any accidents. Going through Étampes, we took on a couple of gendarmes who had been warned and had seen the motor go past without being able to stop it . . . Thirty miles from Orléans the other motor had a puncture. They stopped in the middle of the road and aimed their revolvers at us . . . It was the garage-proprietor who changed his mind first . . . Otherwise we'd have had a regular battle . . . We went towards them . . . The Italian fired a couple of bullets at us without hitting us . . .'

'When you came to my house,' said Monsieur Oscar, 'I gave you a drink. Allow me to observe that it's pretty dry here . . .'

Maigret had had the mechanic brought along from the garage. He looked as if he were counting heads.

'All of you, go and stand against the wall!' ordered Maigret. 'On the other side, Michonnet . . . No need to try getting near Else . . .'

The insurance agent shot him a venomous look and went and stood at the very end of the row, with his drooping moustache and his eye swelling up from the punches it had taken.

Next came the mechanic whose wrists were still tied with electric wire. Then the garage-proprietor's wife, thin and disconsolate. Then Monsieur Oscar himself, who was clearly annoyed at being unable to put his hands in the pockets of his baggy trousers. Finally Else and the Italian, who must have been the Romeo of the gang and who had a naked woman tattooed on the back of his hand.

Maigret looked at them slowly, one after another, with a satisfied smile, filled a pipe, and made for the steps, calling out as he opened the french window:

'Take their surnames, Christian names, occupations, and addresses, Lucas . . . Call me when you've finished.'

All six of them were standing. Lucas pointed to Else and asked:

'Shall I put handcuffs on her as well?'

'Why not?'

At that, she declared indignantly:

'That's mean of you, Chief-Inspector!'

The park was full of sunshine. Thousands of birds were singing. The weathercock on a little village steeple on the horizon was sparkling as if it were made of solid gold.

CHAPTER 10

Looking for a Head

WHEN Maigret came back into the drawing-room where the two french windows were wide open, letting in whiffs of spring air, Lucas was just finishing his interrogation, in an atmosphere which bore a certain resemblance to that of a barrack-room.

The prisoners were still lined up against one wall, but in a somewhat less regular order. And there were at least three of them who were not in the least cowed by the police: Monsieur Oscar, his mechanic Jojo, and the Italian Guido Ferrari.

Monsieur Oscar was dictating to Lucas:

'Occupation: garage-proprietor. Add that I'm a former professional boxer, licensed in 1920. Middle-weight champion of Paris in 1922 . . .'

Some inspectors brought in two new recruits. They were mechanics employed in the garage who had just arrived as they did every morning to start work. They were stood up against the wall with the others. One of them, who had a face like a gorilla, simply asked in a drawling voice:

'Well? Are we copped?'

They were all talking at once, like children in a classroom when the teacher is away. They kept digging each other in the ribs with their elbows, and cracking jokes.

Michonnet was really the only one who kept a hangdog look, hunched his shoulders, and gazed miserably at the floor.

As for Else, she looked at Maigret with an almost conspiratorial expression. Hadn't the two of them understood each other extremely well? Whenever Monsieur Oscar perpetrated a bad pun, she smiled slightly at the Chief-Inspector.

Of her own accord she put herself so to speak in a class apart.

'A little hush now!' roared Maigret.

But at that very moment a small saloon-car drew up at the front of the steps. A man got out, smartly dressed, with a self-important air, and carrying a leather pouch under his arm. He hurried up the steps, seemed astonished by the atmosphere in which he suddenly found himself, and looked at the men lined up in front of him.

'The wounded man?'

'Will you show him the way, Lucas?'

He was a leading Paris surgeon, who had been called in to operate on Carl Andersen. He went off, looking worried, preceded by the sergeant.

'Did you see the look on the doc's mug?'

Only Else had frowned. The blue of her eyes had become a little paler.

'I asked for a bit of hush!' said Maigret. 'You can crack as many jokes as you like later on . . . What you seem to be forgetting is that there's at least one of you who's likely to lose his head when all this is over . . .'

And his gaze travelled slowly from one end of the line to the other. The remark had produced the desired effect.

The sunshine was the same, the atmosphere springlike. The birds were still chirping in the park and the shadows of the trees trembling on the gravel path.

But in the drawing-room lips had become drier, eyes had lost their assurance.

All the same, Michonnet was the only one to utter a groan, a groan so involuntary that he was the first to be surprised and turned his head away in embarrassment.

'I see that you've understood,' said Maigret, starting to walk up and down the room, with his hands behind his back. 'We're going to try to save time . . . If we don't succeed here, we'll carry on at the Quai des Orfèvres . . . You know the place I mean, don't you? . . . Good! . . . First crime: Isaac Goldberg is shot at point-blank range . . . Who brought Goldberg to the Three Widows Crossroads?'

They said nothing but looked at one another, anything but kindly, while over their heads the surgeon could be heard walking about.

'I'm waiting . . . As I've said before, we'll carry on this interrogation at the Quai des Orfèvres . . . There you'll be taken one at a time . . . Goldberg was at Antwerp . . . There was something like two millions' worth of diamonds to get rid of . . . Who started the ball rolling?'

'I did!' said Else. 'I'd met him in Copenhagen. I knew he specialized in stolen jewels. When I read about the London robbery and the papers said the diamonds were supposed to be in Antwerp, I guessed that Goldberg was in it. I spoke to Oscar about it . . .'

'That's a good beginning!' growled the latter.

'Who wrote to Goldberg?'

'She did.'

'Let's go on. He arrives during the night. Who's at the garage just then? . . . And above all who's given the job of killing him?'

Silence. Lucas's footsteps on the stairs. The sergeant spoke to an inspector.

'Go to Arpajon quick and get the first doctor you can find, to help the professor . . . Bring back some camphorated oil . . . Got that?'

And Lucas went back upstairs while Maigret, frowning hard, looked at his flock.

'We're going to go further back into the past . . . I think this is going to be easier . . . When did you set up as a fence?'

He gazed at Monsieur Oscar, who seemed to find this question less embarrassing than those which had gone before.

'There! You see? You admit yourself that I'm just a fence ... And even then ...'

He was a wonderful ham. He looked at the others one by one and did his best to bring a smile to their lips.

'My wife and me, we're practically honest. Isn't that so, ducks? ... It's all very simple ... I was a boxer ... In 1925 I lost my title, and all they offered me was a job in a fairground booth ... That wasn't enough for me! ... We knew all sorts of people. One chap was a fellow who was arrested two years later but who was making a pile just then selling stuff he'd got on tick.

'I decided to try my hand at it too ... But seeing that I'd been a mechanic in my younger days, I started looking for a garage ... What I had in mind was to get the makers to send me motors, tyres, and spare parts, sell the whole lot on the quiet, and then do a moonlight flit ... I was counting on making something like four hundred thousand ...

'The trouble was that I left it too late ... The big firms thought twice before they provided goods on tick ...

'Somebody brought me a stolen motor to be given a new look ... A fellow I'd met in a bar at the Bastille ... You've no idea how easy it is! ...

'That got around in Paris ... I was well placed, seeing that I'd hardly any neighbours ... Ten, twenty of them came along ... Then one arrived that I can still see today, full of plate stolen from a villa at Bougival ... We hid it all away ... We got in touch with dealers in Étampes, Orléans, and even farther away.

'We got into the habit ... It was a cushy racket ...'

And, turning towards his mechanic, he asked:

'Has he tumbled to the tyre trick?'

'Hasn't he just!' sighed the other.

'You know, you look a scream with your electric wire! You only need to be plugged in to make a ruddy lamp.'

'Isaac Goldberg arrived in his own motor, a Minerva,' Maigret broke in . . . 'There was a party waiting for him, because you weren't planning to buy the diamonds from him, however cheap they were, but to steal them . . . And to steal them from Goldberg you had to kill him . . . So there was quite a crowd in the garage, or rather in the house behind . . .'

Absolute silence. He had touched on a sore point. Maigret looked again at their faces one by one, and noticed two drops of sweat on the Italian's forehead.

'You're the killer, aren't you?'

'No! . . . It's . . . It's . . .'

'It's who?'

'It's them . . . It's . . .'

'He's lying!' yelled Monsieur Oscar.

'Who was given the job?'

Then the garage-proprietor, lounging against the wall, said:

'The chap upstairs.'

'Say that again!'

'The chap upstairs.'

But his voice had already lost some of its conviction.

'Come over here, you!'

Maigret pointed to Else, and he had the ease of a conductor who gives orders to the most varied instruments knowing full well that the combined orchestra will none the less produce a perfect harmony.

'You were born in Copenhagen, Else?'

'If you call me by my name, people will think we've slept together . . .'

'Answer me.'

'In Hamburg.'

'What did your father do for a living?'

'He was a docker . . .'

'Is he still alive?'

She shuddered from head to foot and looked at her companions with a sort of vague pride.

'He was executed at Düsseldorf . . .'

'Your mother?'

'She just drinks like a fish . . .'

'What were you doing in Copenhagen?'

'I was the mistress of a sailor called Hans . . . A goodlooking chap . . . I met him in Hamburg and he took me along with him . . . He belonged to a gang . . . One day we decided to break into a bank . . . It was all planned . . . We were going to become millionaires in a single night . . . I kept watch outside . . . But somebody grassed on us, because just as the men were starting work on the safes inside, the cops surrounded us . . .

'It was at night . . . You couldn't see a thing . . . We were separated . . . There were shots and shouting and chases . . . I was hit in the chest and I started to run . . . A couple of cops grabbed me . . . I bit one of them and forced the other to let go with a kick in the guts . . .

'But they came running after me again . . . Then I saw the wall of a park . . . I pulled myself up . . . I literally fell over the other side and when I came to, there was a tall young man there, a real toff, looking at me with a mixture of surprise and pity . . .'

'Andersen?'

'That isn't his real name . . . He'll tell you what it is if it suits him . . . It's a well-known name . . . People who go to Court and live half the year in one of the finest castles in Denmark and the other half in a mansion with a park as big as a whole district of the town.'

An inspector came in with a little red-faced man. This was the doctor the surgeon had asked for. He gave a start at the sight of this strange gathering, and above all at the sight of handcuffs on nearly every pair of wrists. But he was taken up to the first floor.

'After that . . .'

Monsieur Oscar gave a snigger. Else shot a fierce, almost savage look at him.

'They can't understand,' she murmured. 'Carl hid me in his parents' house and it was he who looked after me, together with a friend who was a medical student . . . He had already lost an eye in a flying accident . . . He wore a black monocle . . . I think he regarded himself as disfigured for life . . . He was convinced that no woman could ever love him, that he'd arouse revulsion when he had to remove his monocle and show his eyelid stitched up, his glass eye . . .'

'He fell in love with you?'

'It wasn't exactly that . . . I didn't understand at first . . . And this lot here will never understand . . . It was a Protestant family . . . Carl's first idea, at the beginning, was to save a soul, as he put it . . . He preached at me for hours . . . He read me chapters from the Bible . . . At the same time he was afraid of his parents . . . Then one day, when I was nearly better, he suddenly kissed me on the mouth and ran away . . . I didn't see him for nearly a week after that . . . Or rather, looking out of the dormer window of a servant's room where I was hidden, I could see him walking for hours in the garden, head down, looking terribly harassed . . .'

Monsieur Oscar slapped his thighs for joy.

'It's better than the pictures!' he exclaimed. 'Go on, sweetie!'

'That's all . . . When he came back, he told me that he wanted to marry me, that he couldn't in his country, and that we were going to go abroad . . . He said that he'd finally understood what life was about, that now he'd have a purpose in life instead of feeling useless . . . The whole works . . .'

Her accent was turning common again.

'We got married in Holland under the name of Andersen ... That amused me ... I think I even fell for it too ... He told me some stunning things ... He forced me to dress in different ways, to behave myself at table, to get rid of my accent ... He made me read books ... We went to museums ...'

'Hear that, ducks?' the garage-proprietor asked his wife. 'When we've finished doing time, we'll go to museums too ... And hold hands in front of the Mona Lisa and go into a swoon ...'

'We settled here,' continued Else, talking fast, 'because Carl was always afraid of meeting one of my old accomplices ... He had to work for a living, because he'd renounced his parents' fortune ... To throw people off the scent, he passed me off as his sister ... But he was still worried ... Every time somebody rang the bell he'd give a jump ... Because Hans had managed to escape from prison and nobody knew what had become of him ... Carl loves me, that's certain ...'

'And yet ...' said Maigret dreamily.

Stung to anger, she retorted:

'I'd like to have seen you in my position ... Alone all the time ... And nothing but conversations about goodness and beauty and spiritual redemption and lifting yourself up to the Lord and human destiny ... And lessons in etiquette too ... And whenever he went out he'd lock me up, saying he was afraid I might fall into temptation ... The fact of the matter is that he was as jealous as a tiger ... And passionate too ...'

'After that, I'd like to hear anybody say I don't keep my eyes skinned!' said Monsieur Oscar.

'Why? What did you do?' Maigret asked him.

'I spotted her, dammit! ... It was easy! ... I saw straight away that all her airs and graces were put on ... For a while I even wondered whether the Dane wasn't in it too ... But I didn't trust him ... I preferred to circle round the tart. Don't get all worked up, ducks! You know perfectly well I've always come back to you. The rest was all business! . . . I used to prowl round the house when One-Eye wasn't there . . . One day we got into conversation through the window, because the kid was shut up . . . She caught on straight away . . . I threw her a little lump of wax to take an impression of her lock . . . The next month we met at the bottom of the park and talked shop . . . It was easy . . . She was fed up with that swell of hers . . . She was hankering after the old life . . .'

'And since then,' Maigret said slowly, 'you've been in the habit, Else, of pouring veronal into Carl Andersen's soup every evening?'

'Yes.'

'And going to meet Oscar?'

The garage-proprietor's wife, red-eyed, was holding back her sobs.

'They deceived me, Chief-Inspector! . . . To begin with, my husband told me she was just a pal, and we were doing a good deed by taking her out of that hole . . . He used to take the two of us to Paris at night, and we'd go on the binge with our pals . . . I didn't suspect a thing, until the day I found them together . . .'

'And what of it? . . . A man isn't a monk . . . The poor little thing was wasting away . . .'

Else said nothing. Her gaze was troubled and she seemed ill at ease.

Suddenly Lucas came downstairs again.

'Is there any raw alcohol in the house?'

'What for?'

'To sterilize the instruments.'

It was Else who ran to the kitchen and hunted among the bottles.

'Here it is!' she said. 'Will they be able to save his life? . . . Is he in pain?'

'Whore!' muttered Michonnet, who had been scowling since the beginning of this conversation.

Maigret looked him in the eyes, then spoke to the garage-proprietor.

'What about this fellow?'

'Haven't you cottoned on yet?'

'Pretty well ... There are three houses at the crossroads ... Every night there was a lot of suspicious activity ... the vegetable lorries coming back empty from Paris and bringing the stolen goods ... There was no need to worry about the house of the Three Widows ... But there remained the villa ...'

'Not to mention the fact that we needed a respectable character to sell off some of the stuff in the country ...'

'It was Else, I suppose, who was given the job of fixing Michonnet?'

'What's the good of being pretty otherwise? ... He fell for her straight away ... She brought him along to us one night and we soaked him with champagne. Another time we took him to Paris and had the binge of a lifetime, while his wife thought he was on a tour of inspection ... He was absolutely blotto! ... We told him he could take it or leave it ... The funniest thing about it is that he thought he'd made a hit and turned as jealous as a schoolboy. That's a good one, isn't it? With the mug he's got ...'

There was a vague noise upstairs and Maigret saw Else turn deathly pale. From then on she paid no attention to the interrogation but strained her ears to listen.

The surgeon's voice could be heard.

'Hold him ...'

And there were two sparrows hopping about on the white gravel path.

Maigret, filling a pipe, ran his eye along the prisoners again.

'All that remains to be known is who was the killer ...
Shut up!'

'For receiving, I don't risk more than ...'

The Chief-Inspector imposed silence on the garage-proprietor with an impatient snarl.

'Else learns from the papers that some jewels worth two million stolen in London are probably in the hands of Isaac Goldberg, whom she met when she belonged to the Copenhagen gang ... She writes to make an appointment with him at the garage and promises to pay a good price for the diamonds ... Goldberg remembers her, doesn't suspect anything, and arrives in his motor ...

'Champagne is drunk in the house ... All the reinforcements are called in ... In other words, you are all there ... The problem is how to get rid of the corpse, once the murder has been committed ...

'Michonnet must be nervous, because it's the first time he's been in contact with a real crime ... But he's probably given more to drink than the others ...

'Oscar probably thinks the corpse ought to be thrown into a ditch a long way away ...

'Then Else has an idea ... Shut up! ... She's fed up with living in seclusion all day and having to hide at night. She's fed up with the talk about virtue, goodness and beauty. She's fed up too with her dull life and counting every penny ...

'She's got to the point where she hates Carl Andersen. But she knows that he loves her enough to kill her rather than lose her ...

'She drinks ... She gets bolder ... She has a breathtaking idea ... And that is to saddle Carl with the crime ... Carl who won't even suspect her, he's so blinded by love ...

'Is that how it was, Else?'

For the first time she turned her head away.

'The Minerva, once it has been disguised, will be taken a

long way away and sold or abandoned ... Suspicion has to be averted from the real culprits ... Michonnet in particular is afraid ... So it's decided to take his motor, because that's the best way to clear him ... He'll be the first to complain to the police and make a fuss about the disappearance of his six-cylinder. But the police have got to be persuaded to go and find the corpse in Andersen's house ... And this is where somebody hits on the idea of switching the motors ...

'The corpse is installed at the wheel of the six-cylinder. Andersen has been drugged as usual and is in a deep sleep. The motor is driven into his garage, and his old crock into the Michonnets' ...

'The Police won't be able to make head or tail of the business! ... And there's something else ... Carl Andersen, with his distant manner, is regarded as something of a lunatic by the local people ... The peasants are scared by his black monocle ...

'He'll be accused of the murder ... And everything about the case is sufficiently odd to fit in with his appearance and his reputation ... Besides, once he's arrested, he'll probably commit suicide to avoid the scandal in which his family would be involved if his real identity were discovered ...'

The little doctor from Arpajon poked his head round the door.

'Another man ... To hold him down ... We haven't been able to put him to sleep ...'

He looked harassed, crimson in the face. There was an inspector left in the garden.

'You go!' Maigret called to him.

At that very moment he received an unexpected blow in the chest.

CHAPTER II

Else

IT was Else who had thrown herself at him and was sobbing convulsively, stammering in a plaintive voice:

'I don't want him to die! ... Look! ... I ... It's horrible ...'

It was all so startling, and she was so obviously sincere, that the others, the criminal-looking men lined up against the wall, did not give a single snigger, a single smile.

'Let me go up there! ... Please! ... You can't understand ...'

But Maigret pushed her away. She slumped on to the dark divan on which he had first seen her, an enigmatic figure in her high-necked black velvet dress.

'I've nearly finished ... Michonnet played his part beautifully ... He played it all the better in that he had to behave like a silly little man who, in a case of murder, thinks of nothing but his six-cylinder ... The investigation begins ... Carl Andersen is arrested ... As luck would have it, he doesn't commit suicide and is even released ...

'Not for a moment has he suspected his wife ... He will never suspect her ... He would defend her even if he were faced with positive proof of her guilt ...

'But now Madame Goldberg's arrival is announced – Madame Goldberg who may know who lured her husband into this ambush and who is going to talk ...

'The same man who killed the diamond merchant lies in wait for her ...'

He looked at them one after another, and started talking more quickly, as if he were in a hurry to finish ...

'The murderer has put on Carl's shoes, which will be found here covered with mud from the field . . . It's almost too obvious . . . But the Dane has to be found guilty, or else it won't be long before the real murderers are unmasked . . . There's a general state of panic . . .

'Andersen has to go to Paris, because he's short of money. The same man who committed the first two crimes waits for him on the road, poses as a police officer, gets into the motor beside him . . .

'It wasn't Else who thought of that . . . I'm inclined to think that it was probably Oscar . . .

'Is Andersen told that he's going to be taken to the frontier or brought face to face with somebody in some town in the North?

'Whatever the case, he is made to cross Paris . . . The Compiègne road is lined with thick woods . . . The murderer fires, once again at point-blank range . . . Probably he hears another motor behind him . . . He moves fast . . . He throws the body into the ditch . . . On his way back he'll hide it more carefully . . .

'What matters is averting suspicion as soon as possible . . . This is done . . . Andersen's motor is abandoned a few hundred yards from the Belgian frontier . . . The Police inevitably jump to the conclusion that he has fled the country and therefore must be guilty . . .

'The murderer returns in another motor . . . His victim is no longer in the ditch . . . The traces he has left suggest that he isn't dead . . .

'The man who had tried to kill him warns Monsieur Oscar by telephone from Paris . . . He refuses to come back to a district crawling with coppers . . .

'Carl's love for his wife has become a legend . . . If he's alive, he will come back . . . If he comes back, he may talk . . .

'He must be finished off . . . Nobody has the necessary

nerve . . . Monsieur Oscar has no desire to do the job himself . . .

'Hasn't the moment come to use Michonnet? . . . Michonnet who has sacrificed everything to his love for Else and who is going to be made to take the final plunge?

'The plan is worked out in detail. Monsieur Oscar and his wife go off to Paris, very ostentatiously, announcing the slightest move they intend to make . . .

'Monsieur Michonnet sends for me and shows me that he is immobilized by gout in his armchair . . .

'Probably he has read some detective novels . . . He puts the same cunning into this plot as into his insurance business . . .

'I've scarcely left the house before his place in the armchair is taken by a broomstick and a bundle of rags . . . The trick works . . . From outside, the illusion is perfect . . . And Madame Michonnet, utterly terrorized, agrees to play her part in the act, and, behind the curtain, pretends to be looking after the sick man . . .

'She knows that there's a woman behind it all . . . She's jealous too . . . But in spite of everything she wants to save her husband, because she still hopes that he'll come back to her . . .

'She's right . . . Michonnet guesses that he's been tricked . . . He doesn't know any longer whether he loves Else or hates her, but he does know that he wants her to die . . .

'He knows his way about the house and the park . . . Perhaps he also knows that Else usually drinks a glass of beer in the evening . . .

'He puts some poison in the bottle in the kitchen . . . Outside he waits for Carl to return . . .

'He fires . . . He's at the end of his tether . . . There are policemen everywhere . . . He hides in the well, which has been dry for a long time.

'That was only a few hours ago . . . And during that time

Madame Michonnet had to play her part . . . She was given certain instructions . . . If anything unusual happened near the garage she was to telephone to the Chope Saint-Martin in Paris . . .

'Well, I am in the garage . . . She has seen me go in . . . I fire several shots . . . She turns out the light, warning drivers in the know not to stop.

'A telephone message is sent to Paris . . . Monsieur Oscar, his wife, and Guido, who decides to accompany them, jump into a motor, drive past at full speed, and try to kill me, since I am probably the only person who knows something . . .

'They take the road to Étampes and Orléans. Why, when they could have taken another road, in a different direction?

'Because a lorry is driving along that road which the mechanic has fitted with a spare wheel . . . *And that wheel contains the diamonds* . . .

'They want to catch up with the lorry and then, with their pockets filled, make for the frontier . . .

'Is that all? . . . I'm not asking you any questions! . . . Shut up! . . . Michonnet is in his well . . . Else, who knows the grounds, guesses it's there he's hiding . . . She knows that it was he who tried to poison her . . . She hasn't any illusions about the man . . . If he's arrested, he'll talk. So she decides to finish with him . . .

'Did she slip? Whatever happened, there she is in the well with him . . . She's holding a revolver . . . But he's got her by the throat . . . He grabs her wrist with his other hand . . . The fight goes on in the dark . . . A bullet goes off . . . Else screams, in spite of herself, because she's afraid of dying . . .'

He struck a match to light his pipe, which had gone out.

'What have you got to say about all this, Monsieur Oscar?'

The garage-proprietor retorted surlily:

'I'm keeping quiet . . . I'm not saying anything . . . Or rather I insist I'm nothing but a fence . . .'

'He's lying!' yelped his neighbour, Guido Ferrari.

'Good! I was waiting for you to say something . . . Because you're the one that fired . . . All three times . . . First at Goldberg . . . Then at his wife . . . Finally, in the motor, at Carl . . . Oh, yes! You've got hired killer written all over you . . .'

'That's a lie!'

'Easy does it . . .'

'That's a lie! . . . That's a lie! . . . I don't want . . .'

'You're trying to save your neck, but later on Carl Andersen will identify you . . . And the others will drop you . . . They don't risk anything more than jail.'

Then Guido drew himself up and stabbed his finger in Monsieur Oscar's direction.

'He gave all the orders!'

'Why, you! . . .'

Before Maigret had time to intervene, the garage-proprietor had started hitting the Italian's head with his two fists joined together by the handcuffs, and yelling:

'You little swine! . . . You'll pay for that!'

They must have lost their balance, for the two of them rolled on to the floor where they went on twisting and writhing, struggling furiously, hampered in their movements.

This was the moment the surgeon chose to come downstairs.

He was wearing a pale grey hat, and gloves to match.

'I beg your pardon . . . I was told that the Chief-Inspector was here . . .'

'I'm the Chief-Inspector.'

'It's about the wounded man . . . I think he'll be all right . . . But he must have absolute quiet . . . I had suggested my own clinic, but it seems that that isn't possible . . . In half an hour at the outside, he will come to, and it would be best if . . .'

A howl. The Italian had sunk his teeth into the garage-proprietor's nose and Monsieur Oscar's wife rushed over to the Chief-Inspector.

'Quick! Look!'

The two men were kicked apart while the surgeon, aloof, a grimace of disgust on his lips, went back to his motor and started the engine.

Michonnet was silently weeping in his corner, taking care not to look around him.

Inspector Grandjean came in to announce:

'The Black Maria has arrived.'

They were hustled out, one after another. They had stopped laughing and no longer made any pretence at jauntiness. In front of the police van there was nearly another battle between the Italian and his nearest neighbour, one of the garage mechanics.

'Thieves! ... Apaches!' screamed the fear-crazed Italian. 'I didn't even get the money you promised me!'

Else was the last to go. Just as she was regretfully preparing to walk out through the french windows on to the sunlit steps, Maigret stopped her with a single word:

'Well?'

She turned towards him and looked up at the ceiling over which Carl was lying.

It was impossible to tell whether she was going to break down again or start swearing.

'What do you want? ... It's his fault too!' she said in her most natural voice.

A fairly long silence. Maigret looked her in the eyes.

'Really ... No! ... I don't want to say anything against him ...'

'Go on.'

'You know it yourself ... It's his fault! ... He's half-mad ... It excited him to know that my father was a thief, that I

133

belonged to a gang . . . It was only because of that that he fell in love with me . . . And if I'd become the virtuous young woman he wanted to make me, he'd soon have got bored and chucked me . . .'

She turned her head away and added in a lower voice, almost sheepishly:

'All the same I wouldn't want anything to happen to him . . . He's . . . how shall I put it? . . . He's a good sort . . . But a bit cracked!'

And she concluded with a smile.

'I suppose I'll be seeing you again . . .'

'Guido *was* the killer, wasn't he?'

That was too much. She became the tart once again.

'Oh, no, you won't get me to grass!'

Maigret watched her until she got into the police van. He saw her look at the house of the Three Widows, shrug her shoulders, and scold the gendarme who was pushing her forward.

'You might call this the case of the three mistakes,' Maigret said to Lucas, who was standing next to him.

'What mistakes?'

'Else's mistake to begin with, in straightening the picture of the snow scene, smoking downstairs, taking the gramophone up to her room *where she was supposed to be locked in*, and finally, feeling that she was in danger, accusing Carl while pretending to defend him.

'Then the insurance agent's mistake, in sending for me to show me that he was going to spend the night at his window.

'And finally the mechanic Jojo's mistake, when he suddenly caught sight of me and was afraid the game was up, in giving a lorry driver a spare wheel that was *too small*, the spare wheel that contained the diamonds . . .

'If it hadn't been for those mistakes . . .'

'Well?'

'Well . . . when a woman like Else lies so skilfully that she ends up by believing what she's saying . . .'

'What did I tell you?'

'Yes . . . she could have become something extraordinary . . . If there hadn't been those back-flashes . . . like a summons to return to the gutter . . .'

*

Carl Andersen remained for nearly a month between life and death, and his family, when they were informed, took the opportunity to have him taken back to his own country where he was installed in a nursing-home which bore a close resemblance to a lunatic asylum. With the result that he did not appear in the witness-box at the trial in Paris.

Contrary to all expectations Else's extradition was refused and she was sentenced instead to three years' imprisonment in France, at Saint-Lazare.

It was in the visiting-room there, three months later, that Maigret came across Andersen arguing with the governor, displaying his marriage contract and demanding permission to see the prisoner.

He had scarcely changed at all. He still wore a black monocle and the only difference was that his right shoulder had become a little stiffer.

He looked embarrassed when he recognized the Chief-Inspector, and turned his head away.

'Your parents have let you leave home again?'

'My mother has died . . . I am the only heir.'

He was the owner of the limousine, with a uniformed chauffeur at the wheel, which was standing fifty yards from the prison.

'And you're standing by her, in spite of everything?'

'I'm settling in Paris . . .'

'To come and see her?'

'She's my wife.'

And his solitary eye searched Maigret's face in dread of finding irony or pity written on it.

The Chief-Inspector simply shook him by the hand.

At the county jail at Melun two women used to arrive together on visiting day, like inseparable friends.

'He isn't a bad sort,' Oscar's wife would say. 'He's even too kind and generous ... He tips waiters twenty francs ... That's what did for him ... That and women!'

'Before he met that woman, Monsieur Michonnet wouldn't have wronged a client of a penny ... But last week he swore to me that he didn't even think about her any more.'

At the Grande Surveillance, Guido Ferrari spent his time waiting for his lawyer to arrive with news of his reprieve. But one morning, it was five men who took him away, screaming and struggling.

He refused the cigarette and the glass of rum, and spat in the direction of the chaplain.

MORE ABOUT PENGUINS

Penguinews, which appears every month, contains details of all the new books issued by Penguins as they are published. From time to time it is supplemented by *Penguins in Print*, which is a complete list of all books published by Penguins which are available. (There are well over three thousand of these.)

A specimen copy of *Penguinews* will be sent to you free on request, and you can become a subscriber for the price of the postage. For a year's issues (including the complete lists) please send 30p if you live in the United Kingdom, or 60p if you live elsewhere. Just write to Dept EP, Penguin Books Ltd, Harmondsworth, Middlesex, enclosing a cheque or postal order, and your name will be added to the mailing list.

Some other books published by Penguins are described on the following pages.

Note: *Penguinews* and *Penguins in Print* are not available in the U.S.A. or Canada

CALL FOR THE DEAD

JOHN LE CARRÉ

John le Carré's novel, *The Spy Who Came In from the Cold*, was described by Graham Greene as 'the best spy story I have ever read', whilst J. B. Priestley called it 'superbly constructed, with an atmosphere of chilly hell'. This was no tale of sudden success. The pace, probability, and sardonic humour of his first thriller, *Call for the Dead*, had already placed this author among the market leaders.

It was after a routine check by Security that Fennan of the Foreign Office shot himself. Questions had to be answered; and as George Smiley ('breathtakingly ordinary') prods new facts about Fennan's death out into the daylight, there follows a story which takes an exciting and dangerous course round London and the Home Counties. For Smiley cloaks one of the sharpest daggers in the trade.

'Brilliant new spy story, highly intelligent, realistic. Constant suspense. Excellent writing' – Maurice Richardson in the *Observer*

'Intelligent, thrilling, surprising, makes most cloak-and-dagger stuff taste of cardboard' – Nicholas Blake in the *Sunday Telegraph*

Also available

A MURDER OF QUALITY

POLICE AT THE FUNERAL

MARGERY ALLINGHAM

Starring Albert Campion, bland, blue-eyed, deceptively vague professional adventurer, and Great Aunt Caroline, that formidable and exquisite old lady, ruling an ancient household heavy with evil.

Uncle Andrew is dead, shot through the head. Cousin George, the black sheep, is skulking round corners. Aunt Julia is poisoned, Uncle William attacked. And terror invades an old Cambridge residence.

SIMENON

'The best living detective-writer... Maigret is the very bloodhound of heaven' – C. Day Lewis in a broadcast

SOME OF THE SIMENON CRIME AVAILABLE IN PENGUINS:

Maigret Meets a Milord
Maigret and the Hundred Gibbets
Maigret and the Enigmatic Lett
Maigret Stonewalled
Maigret at the Crossroads
Maigret Mystified

*Also available in the U.K. but not for sale
in the U.S.A. or Canada:*

Maigret has Scruples
Maigret's First Case   Maigret Sets a Trap
Maigret Loses his Temper
Maigret and the Lazy Burglar
Maigret and the Saturday Caller
The Iron Staircase   The Door
Maigret's Memoirs
Account Unsettled
The Blue Room
The Fate of the Malous   Murderer
The Third Simenon Omnibus ★
The Fourth Simenon Omnibus

★*Not for sale in the U.S.A. only*

MAIGRET AND THE HUNDRED GIBBETS

GEORGES SIMENON

First published as *Le Pendu de Saint-Pholien*, this early Simenon records how Maigret unwittingly drove a little man to suicide.

You'd have said that Louis Jeunet was a down-at-heel layabout, but he was packeting up over 30,000 francs when Maigret first spotted him in Brussels. When he posted the money, unregistered, as 'Printed Matter', Maigret followed him for fun. He took a train for the north. At the German frontier Maigret switched suitcases, in a spirit of idle curiosity, but when Jeunet discovered his loss at Bremen he took out a gun and shot himself, and Maigret was left to cope with his own culpability. His subsequent inquiries provoked two attempts on his life and eventually led to Liège, Simenon's birthplace, where in a crazy slum he taps the source of a macabre story which is reminiscent of François Villon.

MAIGRET AND THE ENIGMATIC LETT

GEORGES SIMENON

Pietr-le-Letton was among the very earliest Simenons. It must be the most tortuous puzzle of identities ever handled by Maigret.

Pietr the Lett had for years been clocked across the frontiers by Interpol; he had the personality of a chameleon. Apart from his extraordinary resemblance to the twisted corpse they found in the toilet of the Pole Star express when she drew into the Gare du Nord, he passed as Mr Oswald Oppenheim, immaculate friend of the Mortimer-Levingstons, multi-millionaires; he seemed to be Olaf Swaan, the Norwegian merchant officer of Fécamp; and he was Fédor Yurovich, a down-and-out Russian drunk from the Paris ghetto, to the life. Maigret needed the obstinate nose of a basset-hound to run down this dangerous international crook. He nearly lost his life once and, when they killed his old friend Inspector Torrence, nearly lost his head as well. But he was in at the kill.

SWEET DANGER

MARGERY ALLINGHAM

What was Albert Campion up to in the Hotel Beauregard, Mentone? Posing as the king of a tinpot Balkan state looking for his lost crown. It was all too intriguing for Guffy Randall, so he joined in the treasure hunt...to the bitter end. Even when it got very nasty indeed.